THE FARTHING QUEST

THE FARTHING QUEST

CASEY BRUCE

atmosphere press

1
SPREADING SICKNESS

Most stories start out with a man or a woman who are perfectly happy to be where they are, going about the business of their daily life with contentment. Then they get dragged unwillingly on a grand adventure with amazing new friends and change the world. Too bad this isn't one of those stories. In those stories the hero gets to go back home or moves on to a fantastic new home where everything is great and everyone's happy. I wish this could be one of those stories. My name is Mykall Marshal and, along with my best friend Elion Whickers, I would embark on a journey that would not save the whole world and right all the wrongs but would save my little corner of it. But like most interesting stories, this one starts out in a bar with a man complaining about life.

"Bah, this lot's gone bad in the field. It's useless as anything more than fuel for the fire." Complained an old farmer dressed as if he had just come from the fields as he threw a handful of plants from his fields down on the bar. "Even the cattle and sheep won't eat it, it keeps making them sick." At this declaration, most of the men and women in the bar peered at the plants through the light haze of wispy smoke from all the longpipes in the room. Draveth Mallon poked a tentative finger at one of the stalks before offering the opinion, "It looks as though it rotted in the field." He said of the dark green stalk covered in white fuzz. Several nodded in agreement while others still crowded in for a closer look. A couple of others even drew back a step or two to put a little more distance between themselves and the diseased plants laying limply on the bar.

Very quickly a debate sprang up about the sickness in the crop, whether it was all over or whether this was just an isolated incident in a small little corner of the Farthing Plains. Every farmer and tradesman in the Leaping Toad pub had his own separate opinion and no two agreed. The disagreements over the matter got to be so extreme that it almost came to blows until Draveth stepped in and spoke up in a voice loud enough to cut through the discussions saying, "This bickering gets us nowhere. The only thing we know is that this stuff is in one field. We will have to wait until later in the year to see if it spreads." The conviction in his tone convinced everyone that he must be right so the matter was set aside in favor of lighter talk. As usual, nobody paid attention to the two men in the back, corner table. If they had they would have seen one continue drinking as always while the other watched the uproar with narrowed eyes before turning back to his meal when things died down.

Since the talk was turning to lighter matters it naturally landed on the Midsummer's Eve party. Sitting squarely in the middle of summer, it always happened at a time when all the planting and tending of the crops was finished but before the farmers started to harvest their crop. Every farmer would clean up as best he could and the wives would make their best dish for the feast in the market square. The pub would bring out as much drink as they could spare and spirits would flow in rivers into the cups and down the throats of all the people who lived on the Farthing Plains. The dancing would last into the wee hours of the morning as all of the local musicians took their turn playing so that all the couples could dance while new couples could try themselves out together.

Everyone had a good time as always and life continued much as it always did. One thing did come out of it though: Elion met a girl who was as interested in him as he was in her. The only problem was that her father couldn't stand the thought of any of his four daughters spending their lives with a man without his own land or means of taking care of a family. Since Elion still lived with his family, old man Ruthermon would never agree to let his oldest daughter, Erielle, spend her life with him. The funny part, the part I teased Elion about endlessly, is that because I was careful with my money and good with animals, I already had my own farm and means but no wish to marry at this point. It was one of the only points of contention between us, that I had everything he wanted and needed to marry his girl but I had no urge to marry at that point. While Elion was frustrated, I would always get a chuckle out of his halfhearted laments over the unfairness of it all.

The closing part of the summer was filled with these little bits of heartache and yet more happiness as most of the couples who met at the dance grew closer to each other. No one much noticed the growing number of fields that were being hit with the white fuzz until it was almost time for the crops to be harvested. By that point it was far too late to do very much about it but burn off the infected fields. Everyone had heard about it, along with the whispers of famine and not having enough seed for next year's crop. People started taking stock of what they had in their cellars and most were relieved to find that they still had plenty left there to see them through until next year's crop came in. Then the only thing left for the farmers to worry about was the seed that they weren't getting from this year's crop. Meetings began being held at the pub since that was where all the talking was happening anyway, with the hope that they could get ahead of the rumors still circulating through the town folk about a future food shortage. The pub was the best choice since most of the farmers wound up there each day on their own and after a pint or two people were more likely to be relaxed so things wouldn't get out of hand.

The night after the harvest first began, we all sat down to talk about what we found in the fields. As each farmer got up and reported about his crop, the looks on the faces of the others became more and more grim. Farmer after farmer announced that his crop would be worthless for food and seed while the field would have to be burned and a new crop grown there. The realization rapidly dawned on us that there would not be enough seed to get a full crop in the ground next year and by the end we all just sat there muttering to each other until Elion spoke up. In a quiet voice that went almost unnoticed he said, "If we don't have enough seed ourselves, then we must send someone to get more so that we don't starve next year." I say it went almost unnoticed because only the few people within six or seven feet of us heard him. Several of the men nearby began gesturing for him to speak up when Draveth realized people wanted to hear what Elion had to say.

Once that thought sunk into Draveth's mind in all its import, he shot to his feet to announce the idea and take credit for it himself. In a loud, booming voice he almost shouted, "If we don't have enough seed ourselves, then we must send someone to get more so that we don't starve next year. Whoever we send must leave with all haste once we decide where they should go." As Elion and I were rising to challenge Draveth's usurpation of Elion's idea he moved away from us while still speaking and his lackey Laven hastily stepped into our way to keep us from following. He continued, "These men should be of stout heart and have impeccable character! Humble to a fault! Always willing to put the good of the Farthing Plains above their own! And the most important part," here he paused a moment for effect, "they must go forth sure in the knowledge that their quest must succeed no matter the cost!" At this, all the men stood and cheered for Draveth. Elion and I walked back to our chairs knowing that Draveth had just managed to take full credit for someone else's idea yet again. I doubt that man has had an original thought since birth, as much as he takes ideas from others.

When the cheering died down, a voice from the back asked, "Who should we send? And where should they go?" At this the suggestions started flying and I saw a chance to get even with Draveth for stealing Elion's idea. I stood up and said in a voice that carried over everyone else's in the pub, "I propose that the best man to go on this expedition is the man who first proposed it. We should send such a fine, upstanding man like Draveth to represent us." At least four voices spoke up to second the motion but I thought Elion was going to fall off of his chair laughing at the stunned expression on Draveth's face. For all of his great size, Draveth was rather cowardly when it came to doing new things. The only way he would even attempt to do something like this was with his mousy little toady

Laven nearby. Laven, for his part, idolized Draveth and hung on every word that passed his lips. He and Laven were quickly included in the party much to their chagrin. In the back, I noticed Aereon and Aetheon, the two grizzled old warriors who practically lived in the pub, smirking as they quietly talked amongst themselves. The longer Draveth stood there and listened to people congratulating him on being one of the ones to go the more he glared at me and the redder his face got. Finally, he found his voice and demanded that Elion and I accompany him and Laven. Not many had much to say about that as we were not well known in these parts, but once Aereon and Aetheon saw how the party was shaping up they volunteered to go along to help protect us. I think Aereon's exact words were something like, "We'd better go along too or these young pups will be tripping over themselves while they get lost. It'll be next winter before they make it back." In Aereon's gravelly and rough voice this sounded like the most condescending thing imaginable and most of the older farmers laughed along with the two brothers. As Aereon sat back down, his dark, almost almond shaped eyes glittered at me from under a slightly ragged head of black hair. With that the party was set and it was agreed that we would leave in one week's time.

The next thing up for discussion was where to go. When no one spoke up with a suggestion I looked over to Aereon and asked, "Have you been to any places where they might have enough seed that they would part with what we need?" He looked at me and said, "I know of no place like that where we could go." When he said this, I noticed that Aetheon looked a bit startled and uncertain so I asked him the same question. Aetheon looked up at

Aereon questioningly and at Aereon's reluctant nod Aetheon began to speak.

"Most of the places I've seen in my travels either would not have what you need or would exact too high a price for what they gave you. There is one area that may work though. On the other side of the Forgotten Mountains there are vast valleys nestled in the foothills where they grow the same type of crops you folks do. They would more than likely be willing to help you, but getting there will not be easy. We would first have to ride for many days just to reach the mountains and once there, we would have to face all manner of beasts just to keep moving forward. It is easy to get lost if you are not careful and there are far worse things for a lost traveler than just the beasts hiding in those mountains. For my brother and I it would be no problem, as we have made the trip many times before, but I don't know if you lads have the heart for the journey."

Once he finished I stood and asked a simple question of him. "Is there another way to get what we need?"

He thought for a minute and replied with resignation in his voice, "Not that I know of."

"Then that is the way we must travel." I said with finality. From that point on we knew our course and when we would leave. All that was left was to settle on a means of travel and say goodbye to friends and family.

2
SETTING OUT

As the day we were to leave approached, a collection was taken so that when we arrived we would have something to buy the new seeds with. Each of us already had our own horse and while I had my own wagon, Elion borrowed his father's; between the two there should be more than enough space for supplies and seeds. As we gathered on the morning we were to leave, I looked around at our party and could not help but notice the differences in the way we looked and acted. Elion and I busied ourselves with hitching our horses to the wagons. We had dressed just as we would for a day on the farm with our rough-spun pants, flannel shirts and sturdy work boots. Aereon wore plain armor consisting of metal and hardened leather pieces while he tied his horse to the back of a wagon, then stood around watching all of the preparations with a critical eye. At one point Aereon was asked where his brother, Aetheon, was. At this he replied, "I wouldn't know. Last I saw of him was very late last night when he was halfway through his second cask of ale. He'll show up at some point or other. Sober is another story."

Before he could say anymore, Draveth entered the square from which we were to depart with a great spectacle. The first we saw of his arrival was when an ornate buggy was pulled in by a team of four horses and made a complete circle of the square before rumbling to a stop in front of the crowd that turned up to see us off. You could almost hear the trumpets sound as Draveth stepped out of the buggy and down the two steps to the ground, waving like a king greeting his subjects. He nodded regally in several directions even though no one could tell who he was nodding to. Aereon leaned closer to me and whispered conspiratorially, "Is it just me or did that fool just nod in greeting to the pigs in that pen over there?" At that I could not help but laugh.

Laven ran around like a chicken with its head cut off trying to prepare not only his own equipment, but Draveth's as well, with no recognition but for a few pitying glances and certainly no help. His clothes were quickly becoming filthy but it was easy to see that they had been made with little thought to comfort but much consideration to blending into the background. Laven's quick work got his equipment stored and hid Draveth's as much as anything that garish could be hidden. When all of the preparations were complete we mounted up and at Draveth's imperious hand gesture started off. It wasn't until later that Draveth realized that the guffaws at his hand gesture were because it was a gesture that was generally used to call a halt to the ride.

We set out on our journey with a sense of hope and the cheers of what looked to be most of the town folk and a few of the country folk as well. Elion and I were driving the wagons carrying most of the supplies for the trip. Erielle rode with Elion to the edge of town, much to the consternation of her father. Meanwhile Draveth and Laven rode in front of us and waved like they were going to single-handedly save the entire plain. Aereon rode on the back of one of the wagons claiming he had to conserve his strength and of his brother Aetheon we had not seen hide nor hair all morning. Both of their horses were tied to the back of my wagon so they wouldn't go astray. Finally, we found Aetheon when a great bellowing snore resounded from under the blankets in the second wagon. At first all four of us farmers were scared half out of our wits at the horrendous noise but Aereon broke into a beaming grin and exclaimed, "There he is! I should have known he'd be sleeping off last night's fun somewhere close by."

With the question of Aetheon's whereabouts answered we all rode with a bit lighter heart, the four farmers among us because we now had both old warriors with us and Aereon because he now had his brother with him for the trip. Aereon was in such good spirits now that he jogged up beside the wagon where Aetheon was sleeping and whacked him on the rump with the flat of his sword and a cry of, "Wake up you lazy sot, we're off looking for a fight!"

As we rode, the order of the party slowly started to develop. Aereon and Aetheon rode up front, watching for other travelers along the way and talking quietly amongst themselves. With the nut-brown complexion of their skin they looked as though they spent all day out in the sun, but those of us who knew them were aware that you rarely saw them outside of the pub before closing time. Elion and I drove the wagons to keep them moving along the road. We talked a little but most of the time we focused on the horses and the road. Draveth and Laven brought up the rear, which seemed like an odd choice at first. Shortly after they'd started riding back there Elion felt his wagon shift and we both heard a great thud from it. We looked back and saw that Draveth had heaved himself over the side of the wagon and was settling in to go to sleep, his horse plodding along tied to the back of the wagon.

Elion and I were furious at Draveth for thinking it was appropriate to sleep while everyone else rode and it showed on our faces enough that Laven cowered as best he could behind my wagon. Out of pure spite Elion guided his wagon so that the wheels on the right side hit every rock he could find. After one particularly hard jolt Draveth raised his head and had the temerity to say, "Could you please avoid some of these rocks? People are trying to sleep back here."

That was the last straw for Elion. He threw down the reins for his horse and shouted, "What makes you think you can just get in the wagon and sleep for the whole trip? What about us?" As he talked his faced turned a darker and darker red as his voice got louder and louder. "Do you think you're so much better than us that you don't have to do any riding or work at all?"

Draveth raised his head and fixed a glare at Elion that made Laven duck even further behind the wagon. All he said in response was, "Yes." Then he looked over at the top of Laven's head and snapped, "Come on up and get some rest, too. You may need it later." Then he dropped his head back down and proceeded to ignore us for the next few hours. Laven quietly climbed up in the wagon as if someone had a knife to his throat. Elion was furious beyond words but we both knew Laven was more afraid of Draveth than he was the both of us.

Aereon dropped back until he could talk to both Elion and I. "Let them sleep through this part of the trip. You lads get to see things they will never understand—just look at that view." He said as he pointed off to the west. Off in the distance we could see a jagged line of purple rising up from the horizon. "Those two will never see the Forgotten Mountains this way ever again and you two can drink it all in. You're off for your first adventure and now is the time to see it with fresh eyes." This last part was said with quiet reverence and a bit of longing. He continued, "When those two fools see these mountains it will be after hardships and struggle; you two are the only ones who get to see them through eyes that haven't seen too much. Enjoy it while you can and be grateful those two are at least quiet."

We quietly thanked him and he kicked his horse into a light trot to rejoin his brother. Elion and I just stood there for a minute looking out across the rolling plains of home to the jagged purple teeth of the mountains off in the distance. We were struck with a sense of awe and wonder as we realized that we were almost the farthest from home we had ever been and to accomplish our task we would have to go far beyond the Farthing Plains we called home, with its gentle hills of green grasses and scattered homes. According to the plans we had made before we left, it would be another three days until the rolling hills turned into the foothills of the mountains. As we stood there gazing into the distance I felt a tingle of fear that we were going somewhere I had only heard rumors about. Elion must have seen something on my face because he clapped me on the shoulder and pointed out the two old warriors, saying, "Come on, at least we've got those two. They already know what's waiting for us out there. We'll be fine as long as we're with them." That being said we resumed our trek down the road and toward our destiny.

3
LONG DAYS

What started out as a journey full of hope and the promise of a fresh start for our friends quickly became a long, lonely ride since for the most part nobody talked to each other very much; we just rode along in silence. The mountains grew steadily larger on the horizon the farther we traveled down the road. The longer we rode the more I felt a general sense of the enormity of our task creeping up on us. The mountains in the distance grew from a thin, ragged purple line into tall, grey teeth with a layer of white near the peaks. The first night we stopped after we left home there were three distinct camps set up along the side of the road, each belonging to a pair of travelers. Elion and I set up our bedrolls near a cozy fire that he lit using wood that we had gathered when we stopped to rest the horses throughout the day. We unhitched the horses from the wagons and tied them on long leads to allow them access to as much grass as possible as well as allowing them to drink from the small pool nearby.

Our supper consisted of some greens we found growing in the fields and bread from home. We talked long into the night about various topics, from our journey to the other members of our party. Soon I could not help but comment with a wry smile, "So, if we are successful, do you think Ruthermon will give in for Erielle to marry you?" Elion hung his head and lamented, "I don't think that man would give me a cup of water if I was dying of thirst. He pulled me aside three days ago and told me that I'd better come back with my pockets full or else he would sooner see Erielle an old maid than married to me." I could not help but snicker at that. At Elion's hurt look I quickly explained, "It's not the thought of him not giving in that was funny to me. It's the thought of you waddling into town with pockets bulging out with seed and dumping it all over his head. You could then tell him that you returned with full pockets so you were taking his daughter's hand." He started chuckling at the thought and that set me off again. Soon enough we were laughing hard enough that Aereon ambled over to ask what was so funny and Draveth shot us a disdainful look from the extravagant camp Laven was trying to set up for them. Once we explained to Aereon he cracked a smile and said he would love to see that too. He went on to ask Elion and I about ourselves and so joined our group in talking by the warm, crackling fire. At one point I thought to go ask Aetheon if he wanted to join us but a great, echoing snore from that general direction convinced me it would be a useless gesture.

I was not about to ask Draveth to join us but watching Laven bustle around putting up the huge tent and gather wood to feed the roaring fire almost made me take pity on him. I would have asked him to join us but Draveth kept him hopping by ordering him about to do the work of four men, none of which needed doing but all of which made Draveth feel more comfortable and better about their section of the camp. Finally, Draveth went to bed and Laven almost collapsed where he stood from exhaustion. Watching Laven work, Aereon commented, "That boy wouldn't be half bad if he would stop trying to please that pompous fool and be his own man." Elion and I couldn't help but agree. The problem as I saw it was that it probably would never happen. As the conversation died down to a companionable silence I looked over and saw that Elion had drifted off to sleep and Aereon was regarding me with a questioning look on his face. He nodded to an empty spot near our fire and asked if I minded if he bedded down with us tonight since Aetheon snored to wake the dead. Not seeing a problem with it, I agreed, and we both settled in for what was left of the night.

In the morning, I awoke to a meaty thud and a pained grunt from somewhere off to my left. Aetheon's voice angrily growled, "What the devil do you think you're doing over here, brother? I was counting on you to wake me if something got too close." Aereon's reply took us all a bit off guard when he said, "With your snoring shaking the trees all around us, it's a wonder a deaf person could get any rest. I'd have a better chance of hearing something over here anyway." Aereon then proceeded to cuff Aetheon on the back of the head like he was a small child, causing much laughter amongst the rest of the group.

As we mounted up to start the day, I felt as though we could take on anything in our path. Except for Draveth and Laven, who looked like they were still half asleep and Draveth kept putting a hand to his back. At one point he rode close enough to me that I heard him grumbling about how his back was going to be permanently twisted if he had to keep sleeping on a bedroll. He sounded so pathetic and miserable that I wanted to tell him to hop in the wagon and stretch out for a while, but it being Draveth I just smirked instead and rode on. As he passed the front of

Elion's wagon I saw his horse step in a small hole and give a great bounce causing him to draw up his shoulders and sway hard to the right. I thought I was the only one to notice until I happened to glance at Elion and saw his shoulders shaking in silent laughter.

Our time in the Farthing Plains continued in much the same way as we slowly made our way towards the mountains to face the rigors of winter in the deep valleys that could be found there. The closer we got, the more restless and unnerved I became until the urge to turn back was almost overpowering. If it had not been for the strength and determination of Aereon and Aetheon I don't think any of us would have continued on. It seemed as though whenever the urge to turn back was at its strongest, one of them would be right there to lend a hand or an encouraging word that eased our worries. There was only one evening when these methods did not seem to help. Elion and I were going about our nightly tasks when in the distance we heard a solitary wolf let out a mournful howl. We both gave a start at the sound and Elion, who had been on edge all day, began to look around frantically for his things as he started going on about turning back. I felt much the same way and began packing a few things myself when Aereon came over to us.

Aereon shouted, "Enough! You two are trying to run away like there is no hope and no point to going on. If you are going to turn tail and run, at least wait until it's something worth running from. That out there is just a wolf trying to split us up so it and its pack can get at least one of us. You're trying to make their job easier for them. If we stay together and keep moving, not much can stop us." I couldn't resist saying, "It's that "not much" that worries me." Aereon looked at me scornfully and continued, "The only tough part about wolves is the hide around their neck. It's extremely tough so aim for a spot in front of it or behind it. The hide around the neck is so tough, in fact, that when heated over a fire it becomes as hard as plate mail but will still bend almost like cloth. My brother and I have large sections of our armor made out of this Wolfstrap and if you stick it out, maybe you will earn your own before we part ways." We looked at him doubtfully but continued nonetheless. Elion then nudged me and nodded toward Laven. When I looked in the same direction I noticed Laven watching Aetheon's forearms intently, as if he wanted to ask more about them.

4
FIRST DAY IN THE FOOTHILLS

The closer we got to the Forgotten Mountains the quieter the evenings got. I noticed the group was starting to sleep a lot closer together with a bigger fire between us all. The day before we got into the lower parts of the mountains, Aereon gathered us all together around the fire and told us we needed to start standing watch at night. He recommended we do it in pairs and asked for volunteers to work together. Draveth was quick to volunteer himself and Laven to stand watch together, causing Aetheon to look at them with a suspicious look on his face. Aetheon then piped up that he would stand watch with Elion if Aereon would take a watch with me. It was quickly agreed that two pairs would stand watch a night while the third pair got a good night's sleep. Aereon decided that he and I would stand the first watch tonight followed by Draveth and Laven taking the second watch. Once everything had been dealt with, everyone but Aereon and I settled in for our last night on the Plains. Aereon and I took a walk around the camp to make sure we knew exactly what the area looked and sounded like. We started talking and I learned more about him than I had found out during all of the evenings when we had sat around the fire chatting.

While walking the perimeter I casually asked, "What

was it like where you grew up?" Aereon considered my question while looking at me from the corner of his eye. He was silent long enough that I was starting to regret asking when he finally started to talk in a low voice. "I grew up in a place a lot different than the part of the Farthing Plains where you did, young man. I grew up in Morvale, the capital of Morath, far to the west of the Forgotten Mountains. The only reason I am this far to the east is that this is where my brother and I decided to settle down and retire when our time of having grand adventures got old. My advice to you is to learn all you can about everything so that you can be prepared for whatever may happen. I know I wasn't prepared for anything I had to face; luckily, I had Aetheon with me all the way through or I might not be here today.

"We were born and grew up in a small, two-story home at the edge of town with three brothers and two sisters. Aetheon was always the headstrong one who kept getting us all into trouble either as a group or individually," He said with a small smile, *"while I was stuck being the one to get us out of it. For a while it looked like I would be the one to take over the family shop, with our brothers finding work elsewhere and our sisters being married off to young men finding their own way. Aetheon was the one we all worried about as his first job was tending the bar at a pub and he took to it like a fish to water. It seemed for several years that he would either die behind a bar or under it. All five of us boys had some basic training with a sword and bow but we never thought we would have the need to use what we learned so we mostly took the lessons as something to keep Father happy. That all changed on a winter night when I was only a few years younger than*

you are now.

"There had been a couple of regular army units passing through the area and they stopped to rest on their way through for a couple of days. On the last night before they left, I was walking to my youngest sister Aurol's workplace to escort her home like I had since she'd got the job. She had to pass through a part of town that was not the safest and we all felt it best that one of us boys be there to walk her home. I was running a few minutes behind when I suddenly heard a cry for help followed by a young woman's scream from up ahead. My heart started pounding in my chest as I realized it my sister Aurol crying out and the next thing I knew I was rounding the corner into the alley where everyone had been gathering. As I rounded the corner I saw Aetheon doing the same from the opposite direction and remembered he had said he might be there to walk Aurol home as well." At that point his voice broke and he had to stop to collect himself for a minute before going on.

I could see the tears from old grief welling up in his eyes as he continued, "We both stopped at the raucous laughter from a group of soldiers coming up the alley as they boasted about the sport that they'd had with a girl in the alley. One even smiled as he said that they would have had more fun with her if she hadn't started screaming to the point that they'd shut her up for good. I saw the little yellow flowers embroidered on the dress one of them was carrying wadded up in his hand and remembered how proud Aurol had been the day she had shown us those same flowers after she added them to her favorite dress. Something in me broke at that moment as I stared at those flowers. I took a step toward the soldiers as my hand went to the hilt of my sword and the next thing I was aware of was all six soldiers dead on the ground around Aetheon and I. There was blood splattered everywhere and the crowd was standing back in horror. I distinctly remember seeing a few drops of blood being strewn across the pristine white dress of a little girl and starting toward her to help clean it off before realizing I had been the cause of it when the girl looked up at me in horror as she ducked behind her father's legs. The father looked at me and said he understood why but we had to run or the rest of the soldiers would kill us both when they caught us. I grabbed Aetheon and started dragging him away while trying to snap him out of the trance I must have been in before I came back to myself.

"When we got home, I told my father what had happened while grabbing what I could. He frantically starting helping me gather things while explaining that I had done the right thing and that he would take care of Aurol's body. Mother broke down in tears and started wailing at the news that Aurol was gone. She only got worse when she figured out that Aetheon and I had to go as well. On our way out the door with what few possessions we could carry, Father had to hold her back to keep her from following us down the street. It was the last time I ever saw them or the house I was born in.

"When we managed to make our way out of the city, Aetheon and I wandered from town to town for a while before we managed to find a bit of work with a small mercenary company. At that point I started paying very close attention to the way people fought, both with and without a sword. I learned some new tricks and got rid of some bad habits until I was one of the best fighters in the company. I'm going to start teaching you while we're standing watch once we get into the foothills and mountains whenever we have time. I need the practice and I'll bet you've probably never even held a sword until the day we left." He finished. I nodded solemnly and said I would do my best to learn anything he wanted to teach me. He laughed and said, "To cover everything I want to teach you, we would need to have a girl with us. Lessons in wooing a woman have to be practiced to be properly learned." My face turned bright red at that point from embarrassment. We woke Draveth and Laven when it was time and went to bed. I was so tired from the ride that day and the revelations that night that I fell asleep almost instantly.

It was well after sunrise when I was awakened by the sound of Aereon shouting at Draveth and Laven for falling asleep on watch and letting us all sleep far too late. He quickly got to work packing his bed roll and hitching the horses to the wagons so that we could get started for the day. I roused Elion and we both followed suit. No mention was made of food so I kept my mouth shut and tried to follow Aereon's example. As we all climbed upon the horses and wagons Draveth made for the back of the second wagon but froze in his tracks at a single glare from Aereon. He quickly hung his head and shuffled over to his horse before mounting up; if looks could kill, the glare Draveth gave to Aereon when his back was turned would have struck him dead. When everyone was ready to go, Aereon sent his brother Aetheon ahead to ride point, Elion had his wagon second, Draveth and Laven rode between the two wagons, I followed them and Aereon brought up the rear so he could keep an eye on us all. We had barely been on the road for thirty minutes when Draveth started complaining.

I was just close enough to Draveth and Laven to hear Draveth grumble, "Are we ever going to eat before we get there? Any reasonable person would have had breakfast before we left. I've a good mind to get down right here and not move until we eat."

Laven whispered back, "I'm sure we'll stop soon enough; breakfast IS the most important meal of the day after all."

His voice getting a little louder, Draveth replied, "We should have stayed where we were to eat though. Riding upsets my appetite."

This last was apparently a little too loud as the next thing I knew a melon went flying past me and with a hollow sounding thud hit Draveth squarely in the back of the head, nearly sending him flying from his saddle. Laven barely caught the melon, which had started to split from the impact. Aereon laughed and shouted, "Eat that and quit whining, you big baby! Ask straight away and we'll see what we can do." With a grin on my face I turned to Aereon and asked if there was anything he had that I could eat for breakfast without being brained with it first. With a laugh, he rode forward and handed me some fruit and salted meat before riding up and doing the same for Elion, chuckling as he went. Draveth and Laven were left with the melon that Draveth was hit with.

We rode on in companionable silence for hours on end with the rolling plains slowly giving way to large hills, the low fruit trees dropping away in favor of tall trees and dense forests. Where I was used to seeing rows of crops and fields of grain I was now seeing different colored berries and bushes scattered throughout the trees. Aetheon dropped back to ride beside me late in the afternoon to announce, "Aereon and I are going hunting in the morning. I was wondering if you and Elion would like to come along?"

I could see the sense in it but had a slightly different idea so I replied, "I would love to, but I think you should take Laven with you instead of Elion. Elion can handle Draveth, but Laven won't. Laven needs to learn but that can't happen around Draveth." Aetheon nodded his understanding but said, "We'll discuss it later with Aereon." Then he rode back out ahead of me and stayed there until we stopped for the night.

5
FIRST NIGHT IN THE HILLS

The waving grasses of the Farthing Plains have been my home all my life. The chirping of the insects in the fields of grain have been lulling me to sleep as long as I can remember through my bedroom window. Many nights I have sat on the front porch and watched as thousands of fire bugs lit up the fields with their soft glows scattered around, shining and then not. It relaxes me to see this show. But now I have chosen to leave this place for the good of the Plains. Behind us, the rolling plains begin to glow with the light of dozens of homes and the moon's glow shines down to show us what we have left behind. Ahead the sun is setting behind the jagged peaks of the Forgotten Mountains, looking for all the world like it is being impaled upon the stone teeth to die a painful death. I find myself already missing the vast carpet of straw that grows across the land and longing for the day we return home.

As night settles in, we set up the camp in a small, clear area just off the road. Elion got a fire started while Aereon and Aetheon went hunting for supper. I took Laven with me to find firewood and we left Draveth to unhitch and care for the horses. While Laven and I were gathering wood, I noticed him following me fairly closely and it started to bother me a bit. I turned to him and asked rather roughly, "Why are you staying right behind me? There's no way you can gather up a decent amount of wood if all you're getting is what's too small for me to bother with."

He cringed away from me and timidly squeaked, "I just get nervous doing things on my own. I'm too afraid I'll mess up. That's why I follow along with Draveth so much; he always knows what to do." His words started to tumble out faster and faster along with his voice getting higher pitched until it sounded like metal squealing against metal to my ears.

I finally raised my voice with a shout of, "Enough!" That was all it took to silence him and make him flinch like he had been hit. I immediately felt my pity for him almost outweigh my annoyance once I realized that regular beatings were one of the few things that might make someone cringe so quickly over nothing more than a raised voice. I carefully set down my wood and reached out to gently put my hand on his shoulder while calmly telling him, "It's okay to not be certain what to do at times but I need you to try and work out the best thing to do on your own first. I think you'll find you're better off thinking for yourself. And if you can't figure out what to do, that's the time to ask someone." And almost as an afterthought I added with a smile, "Best to avoid asking Draveth, though. I don't think he could find his rear end with both hands and a map."

Laven chuckled a bit at that and replied with a shy smile, "I'll try. It's just that if I care for him, he'll care for me. Things have always worked out that way, you see." With that he turned away and with a new spring in his step went about thirty feet from me and started gathering wood there. I picked up my load and continued on, feeling a bit better about the journey we were on.

Back at the camp we found a general air of frustration and annoyance brewing with glares being surreptitiously thrown at Aereon by Draveth while he roughly spread the bedrolls. I knew there was something brewing there but I figured Aereon would not hesitate to let everybody know if there was something we needed to hear about. While Aereon and Aetheon were picking through the longest, straightest limbs they could find, Elion had the fire burning merrily with a smirk on his face the whole time. I knew he would tell me later and it would be good. The horses were standing tied loosely to a tree at the edge of camp, happily munching on the grass at the edge of the clearing and drinking from a large bucket of water that Draveth had set out for them.

Sharing the last of the salted meat and some fruits around the crackling fire, Aetheon started talking about some of his past exploits as well as bragging about his prowess as a warrior. I tuned him out for the most part but Aereon's roaring laughter brought me back to the conversation. In the midst of his laughter Aereon cried out, "You only got those four wolves because three were pups and the fourth was the mother nursing them when you stumbled into the den!"

Aetheon stood up and pushed up his sleeve indignantly, "Then where did I get these scars from, if not from the vicious claws on those beasts?" Indeed, there were long, jagged looking scars running up Aetheon's right forearm.

Aereon laughed, "The mother gave you those marks while she was trying to get around her cubs. You barely got your balance back and your sword out before she got turned around. She could have dropped her spoor on you faster than she turned to claw at you."

Aetheon poked his brother in the chest and said with a smug grin, "I still got four Gorlan wolves that night and you only got one and helped with another."

Aereon threw up his hands at that and said exasperatedly, "Fine, have it your way. Next thing you know you'll be saying you killed a bunch of snakes because you fell on a nest and crushed them in their eggs." Everyone but Draveth got a good laugh out of that. Draveth just sat there in the same sullen silence he had been in all evening long. Once the laughter died down Aetheon sat back with his full belly and contented smile, looking around at us before announcing, "I'm turning in and I'd suggest the rest of you do the same. We need to get an early start tomorrow." With that he pulled a blanket over himself and was soon snoring fit to wake the dead.

Aereon picked up four of the long, straight limbs that he and Aetheon had chosen earlier. Sitting to one side of the fire he pulled out a large knife to whittle the end of each limb into a sharp point before laying it aside. While he worked, he caught Laven's eye long enough to ask if he wanted to join us for some hunting in the morning. Laven looked hopefully apprehensive as he explained, "I would love to go but I've never been before." He looked relieved when Aereon told him to stick with Aetheon and to do what he did. Then Aereon handed him some of the limbs before turning back to his work quietly.

The rest of us started getting our things together for bed and Elion finally had the time to fill me in on what had happened earlier. Quietly, he began with, "You'll never believe what happened while you were out gathering wood."

"While Draveth was laying out on a log after having untied the horses to let them roam, I was getting the stones laid out around where I planned to start the fire. I had just gotten the fire lit when Aereon walked back into camp with dinner over his shoulder and nodded to me as he said, "Good work on the fire." Then he looked around at the rest of the camp and I saw a storm start brewing in his eyes. His voice got really low and scary as he asked, "Where is the lazy fool that was supposed to be caring for the horses? We're lucky they haven't wandered off by now."

"Before I could even open my mouth to say a word, his eyes locked on to Draveth and from the look on his face I would not have wanted to trade places with Draveth for all the gold in Jurelle's vaults. I tried clearing my throat to at least give Draveth some warning but he was sound asleep and didn't even stir. Boy, did he stir when Aereon hit him though. I thought Draveth was going to fly all the way across the camp before he hit the ground. Aereon stood over him with his feet planted and shouted, "How dare you take such shoddy care of these animals. We are depending on them to get the wagons through the mountains and back and all you care to do is untie them. I have never seen anyone as lazy as you in all my days." As he stopped to take a breath Draveth found his feet and shouted back, "How dare you hit me! Do you have any idea who I am? I've had horses for years and all I've ever had to do is let them roam. I have servants to finish taking care of them." Draveth took no notice of how red Aereon's face turned at this point. I knew he was about to blow so I busied myself with the fire to stay out of the way. While I was standing there I noticed Aetheon standing at the edge of camp watching his brother go and smiling like he was watching the funniest thing he had ever seen.

"Aereon, however, was just getting started. With a resounding slap, he backhanded Draveth, knocking him to the ground with a stunned expression on his face. Draveth went completely silent as Aereon continued, "I ought to tie you to a tree and let the wolves have you. That way you would have some use as bait to draw them away from us. Maybe you don't get it but if you don't tie the horses close to us, there are any number of animals out there that would be more than happy to eat them while we sleep. They need water and while everyone else is out doing their jobs, they will be tired when they get back. They shouldn't have to do your job as well as their own. If that's what's going to happen we might as well send you back home with your tail between your legs like the lazy coward you are."

"At this last statement Draveth started to straighten up and opened his mouth to respond to the tongue lashing he was receiving. Aereon cut him off before he could utter a sound though, saying, "You don't like that thought much, do you, Mister High-and-Mighty? The thought of being sent back in disgrace is one your ego can't bear. So here's what's going to happen. One, you will do every chore you are assigned and do it to the very best of your ability. Two, you will not try to get anyone else to do your work for you; that includes your toady, Laven. And three, I don't want to hear any complaining out of you during the whole trip, there and back, understood? Break any of these rules and I'll send you packing straight away. Also remember this; we've reached the foothills and the woods. From this point on the likelihood of you making it out on your own goes down each day. After the third day in the woods I'd be very *surprised if you could make it out at all. So you need us more than we need you."*

When Elion finished his tale I wanted to laugh, but, for the sake of the fragile peace in the camp I stopped myself. I told Elion, "Now I wish I had been here to see that. It sounds much funnier than my afternoon." Then I recounted my conversation with Laven for him before we both settled in for the night. My last thoughts as I drifted off for the night were of the fire bugs I could see floating like low-hanging stars, and that after tonight those gleams in the dark might be wolf eyes rather than fire bugs.

6
MORNING HUNT

The next morning the brothers nudged me awake, having already awoken Mykall. Stretching a little, I started fumbling for my heavier clothes which were the closest thing to armor I had. Aereon laid his hand on my shoulder and said, "You don't want to wear clothes that will slow you down or make more noise than they have to, Laven."

I nodded my understanding while changing my choice of clothing. As I finished dressing, I heard Draveth let out a particularly loud snore while he rolled over under his blanket. Since he was starting to wake up I looked toward the food we had available in order to start preparing breakfast until I heard Mykall clear his throat loudly. I darted my eyes toward him as I remembered what he had said about blindly following Draveth around. I realized I didn't want to make breakfast, so I grabbed a piece of fruit and followed the others as they set off into the woods with the bundle of sharpened limbs held in Aereon's arm.

Once we had gone a short distance upwind of the camp, Aereon passed out the limbs and explained that we would be using them as spears and to be careful because we only had the four. He showed Mykall and I how to hold and throw the spear with one hand. Then laying his hand on Mykall's shoulder, he said, "Mykall and I will head North while you two head South. We'll meet back at camp in three hours at the most with whatever we get." Nodding, we split up, and as I hefted my spear, I realized throwing it would not be much different than the Strawfork Toss at the town picnic every year. While I rarely won, I was usually in the top three so I felt a bit more confident as Aetheon said, "Laven, my boy, let's get going so we can show them how it's done." With that we set off through the woods as quietly as possible so as to sneak up on anything out there.

After we had walked for about half an hour in silence Aetheon suddenly stopped and held up the hand not holding his spear. I froze and whispered, "What?" as quietly as possible. Aetheon whispered back, "I heard something up ahead." Then he used his spear to point at a large bird perched on a high limb of a tree about thirty feet from us. He carefully raised his spear into position and said, "Watch this." At the sound of his voice I saw the leaves on a bush about eight feet in front of him rustle as though something was moving in the bush. With no time to warn Aetheon I simply started raising my spear as he threw his at the bird. The throw was made with such force that the spear sailed fifteen feet over the target and knocked Aetheon off balance. As Aetheon stumbled forward trying to regain his balance, his foot landed squarely in front of the twitching bush with a loud crackle of dead leaves.

What happened next was almost too fast for me to follow. At the loud crackle of leaves the bush exploded outward and revealed a wild hog scared half out of its mind. The hog bolted out of the bush and crashed right into Aetheon's legs, knocking him to the ground in a heap, before trying to race past me to safety. It would have worked too if my spear hadn't already been raised. Instead I stabbed downward as it was running past and felt the impact of the spear as it sank deep into the hog's side, pinning it to the ground with a squeal.

It looked as though I had hit something vital as the hog gave two shuddering breaths and died. Standing there resting against the spear I looked at Aetheon just as he looked at me and we both started to laugh. With an embarrassed look on his face Aetheon said, "If anyone asks, that didn't happen. You killed the hog but the rest didn't happen." I stood there with a mix of confusion and humor on my face as I whispered, "Okay." Using my spear, we carried the hog between us as it weighed at least as much as I did. Aetheon walked with a slight limp while I walked with a confidence in myself that I had never really felt before. Since we were the first pair back, there was plenty of time for Aetheon to show me how to clean the carcass and begin the process of preserving it for later. We were talking and laughing quietly while we worked when I noticed Draveth sitting on a log aiming a sullen look at us both. By the time we finished, Aereon and Mykall had returned empty handed but in good spirits. Aetheon turned to me, laid his hand on my shoulder and said warmly, "You did very well today, Laven," loud enough that everyone heard it.

Aereon walked over and said with a smile, "We thought we heard some squealing and a yell; was that you two?" At that I couldn't help but start smiling as Aetheon admitted the truth with a sheepish look on his face. By the end we were all laughing and I had received several slaps on the back. That night the hog was the best tasting meat I had ever tasted.

7

BEFORE THE STORM

Being in the foothills was a completely different trip to the easy one across the plains. The road we traveled was steadily boxed in by steeper and steeper hills on one side or the other. I felt like we were traveling through a new world with unknown perils around every turn. Several times at night we would hear a howl off in the far distance which Aereon said meant that we might face wolves in the near future, but for now they were howling their frustrations at a lack of food to the moon. He also began teaching us how to use our swords more effectively than the old men in the village had when we were boys. The lessons back then were fun and we attended them in order to get out of more farm work. Aereon's lessons now were ones we took very seriously since we were well aware that they might save our lives soon. Since it quickly became apparent that Draveth and I couldn't get along, Aereon started teaching Elion and I while Aetheon was stuck with Draveth and Laven. We would ride throughout the day and then when the camp was set up at night and dinner was done we would work by firelight to become better swordsmen than we had been.

Aetheon was heard shouting at Draveth more often than not while Laven was an eager student. Mostly because Draveth was quite outspoken in his opinion that since he had taken lessons for far longer than any of us, he preferred not to participate in the nightly lessons. Aetheon obliged him by challenging him to a fight the first night of the lessons. If he won, then Draveth would shut up and learn. If Draveth won, he was welcome to sit out or even teach someone if he wanted. Draveth quickly agreed and the rest of us gathered around to watch. The fight was over almost too quickly to call it a fight. Both men raised their swords in their right hands and prepared for battle. Draveth wore his indignation at Aetheon's treatment of him like a new waistcoat and with a cry of rage charged at Aetheon while bringing his sword down in a great slice, trying to end it quickly. If all he wanted was for things to end swiftly then he got his wish as Aetheon swung his own sword in a shorter, lower arc which swept Draveth's own blade far to his left and out of line with any sort of riposte. But Aetheon wasn't done yet. He stepped in closer to Draveth and with a sure smirk on his face swung his clenched left fist into Draveth's jaw with all the strength he had. Draveth straightened as if he was trying to grow a couple of extra inches and slowly toppled over backwards in a graceful arc that was ruined by the way he hit the ground like a sack of potatoes. Aereon stepped over to Draveth's head, pulled his eyelids up so he could see Draveth's eyes and announced, "Well, you didn't kill him. But we'd better let him sleep it off tonight." With that pronouncement, Elion, Laven and I let out a breath none of us realized we'd been holding and closed our mouths which had been hanging open since the fight began. The whole fight and Aereon's checking on Draveth took about a minute in total. All that remained to remind us of the fight was the massive bruise on Draveth's fair skin the next day.

Aereon and Aetheon grabbed Draveth by the hands

and feet to carry him to his bed roll before dropping him on it carelessly. They then rejoined us and Aetheon took Laven while Aereon started teaching Elion and I. That night we focused on basic defenses and our footwork to the point that when we laid down for the night, I felt confident that I would not lose or fall down in the first minute or two of a fight. My lesson continued further into the night than Elion's since Aereon and I had the first watch. Elion was asking Aetheon to teach him more when I finally drifted off to sleep.

The next morning saw all of us but Draveth being a bit more confident as we rode. Draveth hid in the wagon all day trying to sleep off a headache and sulking at being beaten so easily. As the morning wore on and the sounds from the woods became more subdued in tone, our good cheer began turning to apprehension and uneasiness. The bushes seemed to close in around us a bit more and the hills got higher.

Shortly after midday the land around us began to change. The high hills and towering forests littered with low bushes along with weeds that seemed to snatch at clothes and legs at random started to become more scattered the further we went. There was little between the trees but for some roots that grew above the ground. As the tops of the trees grew higher and higher the further we went, a deep sense of foreboding rose up in us. The visible signs were that we all rode a little closer to the wagons and everyone was a little quieter. Draveth shutting up was a welcome reprieve but the hushed tones between Aereon and Aetheon unnerved Elion and I. We traded nervous glances often and gripped the reins for the horses a bit tighter.

As the sun was setting behind the mountains, the shadows among the trees had spread and become quite deep. At one point, we found ourselves looking around at a large clearing as the sun was just a sliver on the horizon, Aereon called a halt to our trek for the night. With a grateful sigh Elion and I began to gather wood for a fire while Laven started dragging out and unrolling bedrolls for each of us. Aereon and Aetheon set out into the woods to hunt for some meat for dinner. With the sense of unease in the air everyone finished their tasks as quickly as possible so that they could get back to the center of the camp. That night, Draveth needed no reminding of how to care for the animals.

While I was out gathering wood I happened to glance down and saw some faded tracks pressed into the dirt at my feet. With a sense of trepidation, I put my hand over one of the paw prints and shuddered when I realized that the print extended past the edges of my hand in every direction. Just looking at the print I knew that whatever made it was larger than I was. Hopefully it ate plants rather than people, but I knew I would be asking Aereon later. I quickly grabbed all of the wood I could carry before hurrying back to the others.

Only after the fire was burning brightly was Draveth willing to come out of the wagon where he had been spending the day with his horse tied to the back. When I asked Aeron about the track I had found earlier he asked me to show him. I took him out to where I had seen it and watched as he started walking around staring at the ground. He occasionally crouched down to sniff at some leaves or the ground before standing up with a loud cracking in his back. He laughed about it and said, "Even my bones object to getting that close to the ground, anymore. As for these tracks," he continued as he waved a hand out toward the ground, "they are several days old. I doubt that these animals are even near here anymore. They tend to move on fairly quickly."

Thus reassured, we made our way back to camp and sat down to a dinner made up of salted pork and potatoes in a stew. Laven had made it with some seasonings he had and we all felt a bit better having had a good meal. The quiet still hung on and it wasn't until I was lying there trying to sleep that I realized what seemed to be missing. The fire bugs I was used to seeing everywhere had almost completely vanished this far into the woods. I had always taken their presence for granted and without them, I felt as though part of the world was missing. I lay there remembering the sight of hundreds of fire bugs blinking on and off out in the fields while I sat on the front porch swing. I remembered the smell of the fresh cut hay drying where it lay before we went out and raked it into bales for the winter months. I wondered if my neighbors were still going by to get what fresh vegetables were left out of my garden for canning. Thoughts of my home and the things going on there lulled me to sleep almost against my will.

8
WOLF ATTACK

The nightly lessons continued as we rode through the steadily rising hills into the Forgotten Mountain range. Often as not we found ourselves going around a large hill rather than over it. It kept the way from being as steep, even as it added miles to our trip. Yet, then with us at night were the howls of lonely wolves looking for a meal! The long, mournful notes were enough to send chills up our spines and make us each scoot a little closer to the fire. By day we would occasionally see a flash of movement far off in the distance that Aereon said might be a wolf or it might be a deer. We always made certain that we stopped in plenty of time to set up camp and care for the horses before the sun dipped below the horizon. The night watches were a lot more serious than they started out as and Draveth never fell asleep on watch again, even though he grumbled about the long nights a lot. We all waited for the other shoe to drop in the form of an attack. It was almost a relief when it finally did happen.

It started out as a normal enough evening with a big fire and the horses standing tied to a nearby tree. The laughter that night felt forced, like we were all trying to be cheerful when someone had just recently died. The normal sounds of the night surrounded us as we ate dinner. After dinner, while we were preparing for bed as well as first watch, was when things began to get odd. When the animals went quiet, the only one who noticed right away was Aereon. It took him hitting his brother Aetheon in the chest with a gruff command of "Shut up for a minute," to make the rest of us stop talking long enough for us all to hear the sharp snap of a stick in the cool night air. Aetheon gathered us four farmers together in a small group and said, "Grab your swords boys, we're about to have ourselves a piece of some wolves tonight!" Upon which he grabbed his sword and set himself beside his brother facing into the dark woods beyond the campfire. The rest of us tried to copy their bravado in grabbing for weapons, but we all stayed huddled together for safety. I caught the eye of Elion and we exchanged what was meant to be a reassuring glance before turning our eyes to the woods in a watchful gaze. Laven not only had his sword but had also picked up the spear he had used to hunt and stood ready to throw it. Aereon quickly reminded us all, "Don't bother aiming for the neck, the hide is tough as armor plate there. Go for the side or the eyes, it's your best chance."

I happened to be looking at one of the nearby bushes and caught a hint of movement in the darkness. Just as I opened my mouth to shout to the warriors, time ran out and the bushes around us exploded in a frenzy of motion and fur as four wolves leaped out at the group. I watched in awe as, with a war cry remembered from long ago battles, both Aereon and Aetheon fell upon a wolf each to begin hacking and slashing with abandon at the tough hides and armored necks in an attempt to avoid being killed. The four of us stood there watching and it was almost too late when we noticed that the other two wolves had circled wide of the fight and were heading straight for us. Draveth screamed, "Run! Into the woods!" in a shrill voice at least two octaves above his normal voice. Elion and I were set to stand our ground there but when Draveth broke and ran we felt we had no choice but to follow.

I lost track of the others quickly and was only aware of the pounding feet and howling of the wolf that had focused on me and was close on my heels. I desperately clutched at my sword as I darted through ever smaller spaces in an attempt to force the wolf to go around. When I got a little bit of distance, I broke into a flat-out sprint in a straight away from the wolf. When I tripped over a limb on the ground, I flew over a small drop-off to land with a sharp pain in my side which caused me to let out a loud cry. The wolf behind me let out a happy yelp as it charged toward me. I looked up from where I lay gasping on the ground trying to get my breath back only to see Draveth running by with a look of stark terror on his face. I held out my hand hoping he would help me up but he just kept running as fast as he could.

Despite the burning in my chest from having the wind knocked out of me, I flipped over onto my rear and started scrambling backwards as fast as I could while holding up my sword in whatever defense I could offer from my position on the ground. When the wolf came sailing over the drop off with its claws out and teeth bared, I froze and screamed, holding tight to the hilt of my sword with both hands. I felt a massive thud and heard a kind of strangled whimper when the wolf hit me at which point I felt this immense weight land on my chest and lower body, pinning me to the ground. I had my eyes squeezed tightly shut and all I could do was scream as I smelled the foul breath of the wolf hit me like a fist in the face. I thought for sure that I was about to feel the sharp teeth of the wolf clamp down on my neck in the next moment, so when nothing happened for a minute, I dared to open my eyes to a most fearsome sight. I was so sure that my next sight would be the open mouth of the wolf coming at me that when I looked and saw the top of its head with my sword rammed to the hilt in its mouth, I couldn't comprehend what I was seeing and could only stare dumbfounded at the sight. The massive beast was panting wildly with a raspy rattling deep in its thick chest, but the shallow breaths quickly slowed to a stop as the animal died. I was in such disbelief that I laid there for a minute just staring at the body.

I was startled out of my reverie when Aetheon grabbed me by the shoulders and shouted, "Are you alright? Are you hurt anywhere?" I was so startled I shouted and flailed at him for a few seconds without thinking about it. He laughed loudly and said, "I'll take that for a no!"

I looked up at Aetheon with wide eyes and in a shaky voice asked, "Where are the others? I know I saw Draveth but I got separated from the others." To which Aetheon replied, "Aereon went to round up Draveth, and the other two found their own way back to camp with their wolf in hot pursuit. Aereon and I killed it since we had already dealt with our own wee beasties. You did a right good job with yours all on your own. I'll have to remember the sword down the throat trick for killing these things." He went on to ask, "Do you think you can make it back to camp?"

At my shaky reply of yes we started making our way back to camp. As we were walking away, Aetheon suddenly snapped his fingers and said, "Wait here." He went back and pulled my sword from the wolf's throat before wiping most of the blood and guts off on the hide of the hulking corpse. He looked up at me and asked, "Do you want the hide or meat from your kill? We have the bodies back at camp, but there's nothing quite like knowing you killed the beastie yourself to spice up the meat a little. This hide is also pretty good for making a cloak out of. This particularly tough section around the neck offers a good deal of protection against most things that might try to poke holes in ye."

The thought of trying to drag the carcass all the way back to camp made my sides hurt just thinking about it so I replied, "The tough part of the hide from the ones back at camp sounds fine to me. I think I bruised my ribs and don't think I could help drag that thing around." Aetheon laughed heartily and said, "I figured that'd be the case. Ta tell the truth I didn't want to drag it back myself either!"

By the time we saw the camp again my sides were burning and I was ready to drop. Aetheon, on the other hand, was still full of energy and upon seeing Aereon back with Draveth, shouted, "We got us a live one on this trip! Killed one by his self by shoving his sword down its throat!" Aereon gave a huge grin and replied boisterously, "We might make a man out of him yet then!" before carving his way into the side of one of the wolves with a long knife he seemed to pull from somewhere in his tunic. Aetheon turned to the rest of us and said, "Here's the way we're gonna do this for the rest of the night. Draveth, you're staying up with Aereon for the first watch. Then, Elion, you have second watch with me. Mykall, you and Laven get some rest. But before you go to bed take a good look at what's left of those critters over there. Those are Morval wolves; they have tough hides but the toughest part is right around the neck.   See where the green fur gives way to the brown, leathery looking part around the neck. You're probably never going to get a blade through it so don't bother trying." Looking over the carcasses, I noticed a large hole in the side of one with the splintered end of Laven's spear buried deep in it. Thinking about what Aetheon said I realized Laven must have gotten in a solid hit but not a killing blow. Laying my hand on his shoulder, I said softly, "Good work with your spear." Laven sheepishly ducked his head, saying, "Not good enough, though." With that I found a semi-comfortable spot near the fire and laid down to get what sleep I could. It was not long after I laid down that I was fast asleep.

9

AFTER THE WOLVES

A sharp pain in my side was the first indicator that it was morning. Unfortunately, I was still stuck in a nightmare of big teeth and foul breath, so when the pain came my mind shoved it into my dream as claws in my side. I awoke with a shout to the laughter of Draveth and Laven, though in the case of Laven it was more of a nervous laugh, as if he wasn't certain he should be laughing. When I opened my eyes the first thing I saw was Aetheon as he looked down at me where I lay and with a booming voice announced, "It's time to get up, Mykall. If you lay around much longer the carrion eaters will think the wolves got you!" Then, while using the toe of his boot to jostle me awake, continued, "Aereon has something for you, along with maybe a little leftover breakfast if you're lucky. Better get it while you can." The smells coming from near the fire made me wonder if I wouldn't be better off missing breakfast.

My curiosity about whatever Aetheon had hinted at Aereon having was enough to get me up and moving about stiffly. I slowly made my way over to the dying fire where he handed me a plate of roasted meat that smelled like it had been over a fire for too long. After letting it cool for a couple of minutes, I tried it, and found that although it was tough the taste wasn't as bad as I thought it would be. A simple question about what it was brought the reply from Aereon, "Don't recognize it? You were the last one to see it alive!" He laughed heartily and slapped me on the shoulder, causing me to choke on the mouthful of meat I was in the middle of chewing.

After I finished my bite of food, Aereon looked at me and held out two pieces of stiffened leather that looked a lot like the bracers that both Aereon and Aetheon wore all the time. When I asked him what they were for he looked at me and said, "Every hunter needs a souvenir from their first kill. These bracers are made from the tough hide around the neck of the Morval wolf you killed. They're stiff enough to stop most things that might want to take your hand off. In fact, I once saw one of these used to knock a sword aside." I looked at them in awe as Aereon showed me how to tie them on myself. Still a bit dazed, I thanked him and walked off rubbing my brand-new bracers, feeling the hard, stiffened leather. I could smell a bit of the earthy, leather smell and hear the creak as it shifted around my forearm.

Elion and Laven could not take their eyes off this mark of respect from the two old warriors. Draveth took one look at them and with an unimpressed tone said, "They smell funny, and it'll probably get worse over time," before walking off again.

Aetheon walked up behind me and laid his hand on my shoulder. "Don't give him another thought," he said. "That fool will probably never earn anything like that in his entire life. It's the mark of a man that'll do what he has to, even if he's scared. That fool will just run screaming like a little girl." Having said his piece, Aetheon walked off and tossed a final comment over his shoulder. "Let's go see what other hardware you can earn, eh!"

I pulled Aereon aside and in a quiet voice said, "I feel

like I don't deserve these. I didn't even know I had killed it at first—my eyes were closed. I just held my sword out hoping to scare it off."

Aereon looked at me and smiled widely, saying, "That's the thing, though. You didn't turn to try and run like that fool Draveth. He could have gotten all of you killed." I thought for a moment of the look of terror on Draveth's face while he ran from the wolves and had to admit that Aereon had a point. He continued, "Being brave is not all about standing tall while hacking and slashing at everything that comes your way. Sometimes it's about doing what you need to do even when you're scared to death. You held onto your sword until the end and you were the one who survived. That right there is enough to earn these, as a Morval wolf does not die easily. Next time you'll know you have the strength to stand in the face of your fear." I felt a bit better after that. I realized at that point that I had done something the others had not.

With half the morning gone we hitched the horses and mounted up to ride as far as we could through the snowy forest nestled in the mountain valley. I sat a little straighter upon my horse as we rode and felt as though I could take on anything that day. The crisp, cool air smelled a bit cleaner and it felt as though my horse had a bit more spring in his step. I knew things were going to get better from there on out. It made the grandeur of the valley that much more impressive when we came out of the woods on top of a bare spot partway up the face of the mountain. Looking across the valley, I could see signs of small huts dotting the hillsides and the gleaming of the meandering river as it made its way through the valley towards the lakes. I spotted the slate-gray stone of the city just as Aereon gave a small cry of, "The city of Hodswell; if we hurry, we'll spend tonight in a soft bed at the inn." We all drove the horses a little harder at the thought of a good meal and a soft bed. But by the middle of the afternoon we knew that we were going to be spending another night camped out, based on how far from the city we were.

That realization was enough to cast a pall of unease across our group as everyone remembered what had gone on the night before. We pushed as far as we could before stopping, even though we were still more than half a day's ride from Hodswell as the sun was dropping below the horizon. Aereon had us build the fire right beside the road and leave the horses hitched to the wagons just in case we needed them in a hurry. No one slept much that night and each of us was glad to get on the road the next morning. Draveth, oblivious as always, whined about breakfast when Elion put the fire out as soon as the sun came up. The rest of us were already putting away all of our gear so we could get going. We all just ignored Draveth and continued about our business.

While we rode, Elion and I carefully watched the road ahead of us while the others watched everything around us. By midmorning we could see how close we were getting to the city and the mood started to lift. Aetheon started telling us stories about his friend Erog, who lived just outside the city and ran a pub near the center of the city. By the third story, most of us had tuned him out. Laven was the exception; he hung on every word out of Aetheon's mouth as though his life depended on it. Elion, Aereon and I found it funny, but Draveth started out looking annoyed and then downright angry as he saw his hold over Laven diminishing more and more. The further we rode, the more houses we saw. Each one was empty and looked as though nobody had lived there for months, if not years. Finally, one house came into sight that caused Aetheon to kick his horse into a full gallop. I looked questioningly at Aereon who simply said, "Erog's home." I nodded my understanding and continued on as I had been. Soon enough, we caught up with Aetheon and dismounted to see what he had found.

10
THE HOUSE OF EROG

At the hut, Aereon climbed down from his horse to look around inside and when we followed him in, he looked at us all and in a grim tone observed, "We knew the family that lived here and they would not have simply abandoned their home for no reason. They would have fought for it to the point that we would find their remains strewn about."

Draveth looked unsettled as he tried to find an explanation. "Maybe they were up against something they knew they couldn't beat," he said in a quavering voice, "or the land turned bad so they left before all the destruction happened."

"No," Aetheon assured them, "they wouldn't have left their home even if the land turned. They would have stayed and found something else to do for their livelihood. They were killed or driven off. Only question is, what could have done all this and not left any evidence?" He threw down the broom he had been looking at as if it might come to life and tell him what had happened to his friends if he hurt it. The grief and worry on his face was almost overwhelming as he sat heavily on a chair. As Aetheon sat there, it looked as though he aged five to ten years because of the weariness on his face. I walked outside with Aereon to take a look around outside.

As I explored around the house, it looked like how a typical farmhouse and yard on the Plains would. The only thing missing was the people; even the animals looked right at home. I met back up with Aereon, who had also found nothing, and as we looked around I wondered why this one place had affected Aetheon so much. I asked Aereon why and with a great sigh he sat on a log and began to tell me a story from his and Aetheon's past.

"*Many years ago Aetheon and I roamed these mountains among other lands looking for fame and fortune fighting other's wars for them. We were leading a company of men and women through a pass that runs north of here so that we could reach the western slopes of Mount Horowin as quickly as possible. There were rumors that a group of dark faeries known as the Grimm had an enclave there with a treasure trove like none had ever seen before. We were bound and determined that the treasure would be ours, even if we had to kill every last Grimm to get it. We started out with thirty in all, strapping men and women who we knew from personal experience to be good in a fight. When we made it to Hodswell, we decided to stay and rest for a couple of nights at The Lucky Bucket before pushing on. We had such a good time here that three of our number almost stayed behind to settle down. It was only our oaths to each other and the promise of a massive payday that kept the company together long enough to get moving again.*

We made it through the pass and started across the western slopes looking for the landmarks described on the map we'd found in a dusty old book sitting on a library shelf. At first we almost missed the side trail that led to the Enclave, it was so overgrown with bushes and vines. If not for the stone marker set beside the trail to warn people away, we would never have found it. In many ways, I wish we hadn't found it, then so many would have lived. Instead, only a few made it out.

The trail was a hard one to follow; we had to hack our way through vines and dodge fallen trees as big around as a cart's wheel. We were fortunate enough to make it to the Enclave while it was still mid-afternoon and took a little time to look around and find a way in. Finally, we gave up and simply hacked our way through the door locks to make things easy. Mykall, my boy, you should have seen it! There was gold and jewels everywhere the eye could see. We spread out and quickly loaded up our bags with everything we could carry. I myself found a diamond encrusted tiara to go along with piles of gold coins and precious jewels. After we had spent a good hour or two sorting the loot and packing what we could carry, we set out back along the trail at a leisurely pace, talking and laughing about the ease of the whole thing. We gave nary a thought to the time of day, since we hadn't seen anyone at the Enclave. That was where we went wrong. Had we given any thought to the matter of the Grimm being dark faeries, we might have realized that they only come out when the sun is down.

The first sign that something was amiss came just as the sun dipped below the horizon in the form of an unearthly wailing that rang out across the mountainside. We all stopped as we heard that inhuman wail start up and looked around frantically for any sign of the cause. When there was no sign of anyone out there, we looked at each other with wide, frightened eyes as we stood there listening to the ominous stillness that lay all around us like a thick blanket. As one, we began to run down the trail, clambering noisily over any obstruction in our way. There was shouting from all sides as the wailing came right up beside the company as we ran. The most terrifying part of the whole thing was that we were running in almost perfect darkness and tripping over trees and rocks, but the things out there in the woods had no such difficulty.

The shouting was quickly joined by screams from those who fell but, those screams were abruptly cut off soon after they started. The whole thing was so surreal that it seemed like we were having a collective nightmare, but for the pain of branches hitting us that we had pushed aside on our way in that afternoon. When we reached the point where the trail met the main road we gathered those of us that were left into a rough circle with Aetheon in the center trying to light a fire so we could see what we were trying to fight. While the light was still a flickering little flame we couldn't see much, but since we had stopped running, we could hear the thud of a person hitting the ground, then a long, high-pitched scream that faded into the distance before being abruptly cut off. By the time Aetheon got the fire blazing so we could see, there were only six of us left out of the original thirty who had set out that morning. As we stood with weapons drawn, facing outward, I saw a sight I will never forget until the day I die. That thing's face was long and would have been hauntingly beautiful had it not been for the inch-long fangs dripping with the blood of my friends. High, prominent cheekbones matched with thin, delicate lips that were dominated by soulless black eyes that made you feel as if you were sucked in if you stared at them for too long. As I stared at it and it stared back at me, one long arm reached out to wrap its claws around my ankle so as to drag me into the night. In a panic, I swung my sword as hard as I could and took its arm off at the shoulder, causing it to let out a piercing shriek and turn to flee back into the woods.

Having hurt one of them, I felt good about my chances against the others, so I turned to find another just in time to see one of them jump on Karyana, the last woman standing. I watched as though in slow motion as its head dove forward at Karyana's throat and latched on with those long, sharp teeth. Karyana let out a wet gurgle; she died while I swung my sword around in a flat arc. The Grimm looked up in surprise just in time for my stroke to take its infernal head off. The loss of two of their own put the dark faeries back on their heels for a minute, which was just long enough for Aetheon to scatter torches around us. The light and heat seemed to drive them back somewhat, so we built up fires as best we could and hunkered down behind the flames to wait out the night. The wailing continued throughout the night just beyond the light of the fires and made sure that none of us slept a wink. When the sun heaved its way over the side of the mountain, those things were gone as fast as they had come. We looked around ourselves in disbelief at our survival, but quickly agreed that we needed to get moving lest we be caught out at night again.

When we finally made it back to Hodswell, the five of us decided to stay until we had recovered our strength enough to move on. Two weeks had passed before we all felt ready to move on. My brother and I decided to leave the mountains and retire to the Plains where we could live out our days in comfort with the loot we had taken from the Enclave. That was where we stayed until we were recruited to help four young men cross the mountains and get back again. Karyana's brother, Kaylor, couldn't live *with the memory of his sister dying, so he gave his treasure to the rest of us the night before we found him hanging from the ceiling in his room. It turned out Garthog hadn't escaped as unscathed as we all thought and his leg quietly got infected. By the time anyone but Garthog noticed, it was already too late for him to survive, despite the local doctor's best efforts. Finally, Erog met a local girl and decided to stick around and buy a small spread to raise a family on. That's where we are right now."*

When he finished his story Aereon gave out a great sigh and heaved himself up with a grunt. We both headed back inside and, after talking with the others, agreed that we should stay at Erog's house that night so that we could lock the door and have warm beds to sleep in. My last thought before I dozed off was to hope that whatever had happened here would not happen again.

11
THE RUIN OF HODSWELL

When morning came upon us, it dawned with a wan light on a light coating of snow that was spreading across the valley. The only breaks in the sheet of glistening white were where the trees from the forest poked up and the massive grey stones of a city looked to be deserted and crumbling from disuse. Even from miles away we could see three places where the outer walls had crumbled and one corner of the keep had simply vanished behind the inner wall. The entire city was silent as a tomb from the time we got close enough to be able to hear the skittering of a few rodents until we were deep into the narrow streets. Without even realizing it, we all rode a bit closer together and stayed in the middle of the empty cobblestone streets as though the abandoned shop fronts would grab us and drag us away.

As we pushed on into the city's square marketplace, Aetheon rode over to a sign and stopped. He dismounted and slowly made his way inside as though that one place was all that existed in the world. I accompanied Aereon as he rode closer and shouted, "Hurry up, you fool! I don't want to be anywhere is this accursed place when that sun goes down." I started to smile at that but stopped and lost the bit of good cheer when I noticed the sign out in front of the place said 'Erog's'. Since the place was as barren as the rest of the town, I knew that Aetheon was not likely to find his friend anytime soon. It looked as though I was right when Aetheon slowly shuffled out the front door and with a melancholy gaze at the sign climbed up on his horse and wheeled it around towards an exit from the square.

The entire time we were in the city, I had the strangest feeling that we were being watched. It was strange because while we were getting to the market, and for a while beyond it, I saw nothing to indicate there was anyone else around. It was when we passed by an abandoned tailor's shop that I happened to glance up the alley beside it to see a pair of eyes set in a small face peering around the corner of the shop from the back. The face the eyes belonged to was round and dirty but full grown even though it looked as though the person couldn't have seen more than twenty summers. I was in the rear of the party so it was easy for me to slip away unnoticed and ride up the alley to investigate. Sadly, as I got closer, she moved further away, so I was never able to get a good look at her. What I could see was unique in form and colors. She, and I was certain it was a she, had an exotic or almost cherubic look to her. The eyes looked purple from a distance and there almost seemed to be a bit of a point to her ears, just like a faerie. I had no idea what her voice would sound like but I thought it must be musical just from the look of her.

I tried calling out, "Hello? Can I talk to you? Do you know what happened to all of the people here?" as I jogged up the alley toward her. My approach only seemed to spook her even more as she turned and ran up the alleyway before disappearing into a doorway set back into the wall. I rode there as fast as I could but all I found was a locked door to a shop with only a few high windows that were unreachable for me. The whole of the incident troubled me for the rest of our time in Hodswell. Still thinking over the odd meeting, I caught up with the rest of the group and rode slowly through the city, following the others as if in a trance. The thought kept rolling through my mind over and over, wondering just how long she had been watching us and why she was there. All I knew was that once I saw her and she ran from me, the feeling of being watched faded away quickly and never returned. It was only when we were well clear of the city that I felt comfortable enough to ride up to Aereon and tell him everything I saw in the side street. He looked thoughtful for a few minutes and then said, "I suppose she must have been a traveling scavenger and just happened to notice us passing through."

I wondered aloud, "Will she follow us outside of the city?" A part of me hoped he would say yes, while another part of me hoped he would reassure me she would not. Instead he chose the most frustrating option and told me that she might or might not depending upon how easy the road was and how interesting she found us. As it was, I could not catch another glimpse of her and as we rode past the wall and further down the road, the feeling of being watched slowly faded away. Try as I might to forget those beautiful eyes, I knew they would haunt me for some time to come. What I could not have known was the part that the owner of those eyes would play in the days to come.

The road out of the city forked within a couple of miles of the city, with one fork circling high up on the side of the mountain and the other turning to the right to drop down into the valley. When we came upon it, Aetheon and Laven were in the lead with Draveth riding beside Elion which left Aereon riding alongside me. Aetheon paused when he got to the fork and waited for Aereon to catch up so that they could have a talk away from the rest of us. After a bit of quiet arguing and pointing at each road, Aetheon started off down the right fork into the valley below to face the snow that was beginning to come down harder. Aereon waited as first Laven, then Draveth and Elion took the right fork. When I was moving past he fell in beside me. Since he was within easy talking distance I asked, "What was all that about?" Aereon grunted and replied, "We just needed to decide which way to go. The left fork is much shorter but holds dangers you lot are not ready to face. On the way, back we may be forced to take it, but I don't want to chance it unless we have to. The way we're going takes twice as long but it's open country almost all the way through. We'll take this road through the base of the mountains and, once we cross the river, we just have to make it through the Northern Pass and we're on the other side. Another two weeks of travel and we start looking to buy seeds."

Still a bit curious I asked, "What lies down that other road?"

With a grim set to his face he told me, "A couple of miles down the road there is a fork that leads to a cave where live some of the foulest things ever known. If you don't take that particular road to ruin, then ten miles on you follow a curve over the shoulder of Mount Vargul and quick as can be you're past the mountain range. If you can take the road quickly enough to stay in the light of day, you stand a chance of being left alone. But if you lose the light, then abandon all hope because you're probably dead." He threw his head back with a laugh at the look on my face and said, "That's why we're not going that way." When I asked him if he'd ever been down that road before he said, "Once, and never again."

With that ominous warning I counted myself lucky that we were going down the right fork and kept my mouth mostly shut for a while. Anything that would make someone like Aereon or Aetheon nervous about a road was not something that I wanted anything to do with. The further into the valley we rode, the deeper the snow got until it was ankle deep. The horses and wagons had no problems continuing on, but if it got deeper before we went back home then we would be in a heap of trouble. Thankfully, the road was well marked so there was no danger of losing our way in the snow.

It took us six days to make it through the valley, but thankfully the unsettled feeling that I felt at the thought of the other road went away after the first day. By day, the sun reflecting off the snow was nearly blinding and by night, the new moon meant that the only light was what came from the stars that reflected off the snow and the light from our fire. It was quite beautiful at night and got even better when the moon started growing again in the sky. The lack of new snowfall also meant that what was on the ground began to melt when the sun was high.

Problems came as we began to approach the river and the mountains it flowed between. Looking out across the water, it seemed as though it would be fairly easy to cross, but Aereon warned us that it would be difficult the farther out we were. About a third of the way across, Laven's horse balked at the depth of the river and reared enough that he was flung off into the water. When Laven was thrown, he was forty-five feet upstream from my wagon and around thirty feet further out so I had a clear view as he broke the surface and lost his bearings. He began flailing and spluttering so badly I feared he would drown so I urged my horse ahead to get the wagon close enough that he could reach it. My aim was true but Laven's desperate grab for the side of the wagon missed. At the last possible moment I leaned to the side in order to reach down and pull him from the water. Laven clutched at me as if his life depended on it, which had the effect of soaking me to the bone in the water that was weighing his clothes down. I got him into the wagon and got back to the reins before my horse panicked so I was able to get us safely to the far side. Laven's horse, once unencumbered by a rider, followed meekly along behind my wagon all the way across and up the far bank. As Laven huddled under a dry blanket as close to the center of the wagon as he could, I heard a muffled, "Thank you," come from within the blanket. While we all made it across safely, the good mood that was present before the river had been thoroughly washed out of us by the freezing cold water. What arrived in its wake was a more cynical view of our chances. The foreboding feeling started to return despite the warmth of the evening fire.

12
THROUGH THE SNOW

The melancholy mood left behind after the river crossing was not helped in the slightest when we awoke the next morning to find that the weather had turned on us and started dumping snow in the night. The snow, which until that point had melted down to about three inches deep, was now nearly halfway to my knees and still growing. As we were packing to go, Aereon said, "Best be getting along; the pass itself will only get worse." Then he fixed each of us with a sharp look and said, "Make as little noise as possible. Some parts of the pass are unstable enough that a loud enough noise will bring all the snow on that side of the mountain down around our ears." All of us looked thoughtful at that except for Draveth, who scoffed and said, "Frightful old man, it can't happen that way," as he mounted his horse to go. The rest of us quietly mounted up and started off for the day, afraid for what it might bring before nightfall.

As we pushed on through the snow, I looked around at the desolate field of white and my heart sank further into my chest. Surely there was no way we could make it through this frigid gap alive. The white peaks around us seemed to close in and mock us with their looming presence as they towered above us. I looked ahead at Elion and sought strength in his gaze but there was none there to be found. He looked back at me then hung his head and in a sorrow-filled tone said, "My toes have forgotten what it is like to be warm. Even if we make it, I don't think they will ever be warm enough for me again." I could not help but agree and turned dejectedly back to my contemplation of the sheet of white all around us.

Had it just been myself that was making this trek, I would surely have turned back at once to seek a different path. The gray, bleak sky that dropped more snow on us throughout the morning only served to increase my despair. The snow continued to get deeper, making the trip harder for the horses and causing us to move ever slower as we pushed on through the drifts. Gradually, the way began to rise as we made our way up the massive shoulder of a mountain and the snow drifts started to thin the higher we went. Our relief at the easier travel was cut short, however, when Elion's wagon slid sideways and one of the wheels dropped off of the roadside. There was a frantic scramble to keep the rest of the wheels from sliding further until Elion could turn the horse toward the mountain side of the road and away from the drop off. None of us knew how far the drop was but none of us wanted to find out either. Finally, the horse managed to pull the wagon back up completely on the road and we were all able to breathe a sigh of relief. Naturally, Draveth could not resist saying, "Try to watch where you're going next time; if it happens again, we might just save ourselves the trouble and let you fall." Laven bristled a bit at that and Aetheon looked like he was about to say something when Elion said through gritted teeth, "Why don't you ride to that side of the wagons so we'll find the drop off beforehand. That way we won't lose anything important." At the furious but stymied look on Draveth's face, everyone had a good laugh, even Laven, and you could feel some of the tension melt away from most of us. Draveth continued to seethe and mumbled under his breath, "We'll see who's laughing by the time we get back home." I shot a quick glance his way but said nothing as I was the only one to hear.

With every hour that went by with no other incident the mood lightened until, by late afternoon, we were all feeling a bit better about our odds of making the trip to the Golden Plains and back home. By this point, the side of the mountain was getting higher above us so when Draveth got it into his head to start whistling, Aereon rode up beside him and slapped the back of his head, hard. In a quiet voice, just barely loud enough for all of us to hear, he cautioned, "Keep your lips together; we don't want the side of the mountain to come down on us." While the rest of us nodded solemnly, Draveth mutely glared at Aereon's back, as if imagining a knife buried there. This look was not lost on Aetheon, who rode up to Draveth, much as his brother had, and slapped the back of his head harder than Aereon had even thought about hitting him. At Draveth's sharp glare, Aetheon shrugged nonchalantly and said, "If you even think about trying it, it will be a toss-up as to which of us kills you before you can lay a hand on either of us." Then he laughed softly as he rode away.

As the day drug its way along, the sun poked its way through the clouds and shone down, causing the snow to shine brighter than a blazing fire in the night. I stopped and stared at the sight and didn't look away until Aereon thumped me on the shoulder and cautioned, "If you keep staring at it like that, you'll go snow blind in short order. Best to look at what's in front of you and then pop your head up occasionally to look around. Best way to see it all without tripping over your own two feet." When I looked away from the snow in the valley, I could tell what he meant since I could barely see anything other than big, bright, purple blotches everywhere I looked. After those spots cleared, I was careful about how long I looked at the valley floor and the mountains that rose tall in the distance. Soon, though, it was time to stop for the night and make camp. We separated out to our usual duties which for Laven and I meant digging through the snow to find what firewood we could. Pickings were slim and what we could find was wet enough to be trouble to burn. Elion managed though and we were soon warming ourselves by the fire and eating the furry hopping things that Aereon and Aetheon killed when they burst into a run across the surface of the snow. The things were quite tasty and when I asked where we could find them on the Plains, the two warriors said they were everywhere and ate our gardens if we weren't good stewards of our fences. As the conversation wound to a close, most of the eyelids around the camp had started to droop, heavy with weariness.

As the others were getting settled in for the night, Aereon called me over to him and we made our way to the side of the road overlooking the valley floor. As we approached, he threw his arm over my shoulders and said, "This is the proper way to see snow." With that he waved his other hand in a broad gesture that encompassed the view ahead of us. Where the moonbeams pierced the clouds the entire valley before us appeared to glisten like ten million stars that all fell to one small part of the earth at the same time. I stood in awe at the sight and whispered, "It's the most beautiful thing I think I've ever seen." I knew I was standing with my jaw gaping open but

I had neither the ability nor the desire to close it since that would mean focusing on something other than the sight before me.

Aereon stood there grinning with that self-satisfied grin I had seen on his face before and whispered back, "There be things out there that are far lovelier than this. But there's not too many of 'em." Then he walked quietly back to camp, leaving me to gaze out into the night in wonder. My last thought before I fell asleep was to imagine how much I had yet to see. My dreams that night were filled with specks of light that swirled around each other before scattering across the landscape and the night sky equally. But just as I felt the call of wakefulness dragging me from slumber, I thought I saw two purple lights close to where I was. And below them, a secret smile that stretched almost out to two slightly pointed ears. Why I would dream of that I do not know, but it didn't feel frightening; in fact, it felt quite nice.

The night passed quietly and in the morning we all awoke and packed to go after eating the leftover food from dinner the night before. It had been perfectly preserved by the cold snow and was easily warmed by what was left of the fire before we put it out. By mutual agreement, Elion and I each kept a blanket out to wrap ourselves in as a bit more protection from the cold. Aereon and Aetheon broke out heavy fur overcoats and Aetheon even had an old, smaller coat stashed in his things that he brought out for Laven. When Draveth asked about one for himself, the brothers just shrugged and said in unison, "Didn't think to bring extras for everybody. And don't even think about a blanket; it'll get your horse all tangled up." Draveth asked, with a bit of petulance in his voice, "Then how am I supposed to stay warm?"

Aereon thought for a minute and dug in his pack before throwing a bundle of heavy cloth at Draveth, saying, "Put these on, they'll keep you warmer. Just make sure they stay clean and in good repair or I'll take it out of your hide." I looked over at Aetheon while Draveth was getting dressed and asked, "What are those?" Aetheon snickered and told me, "Aereon's long underwear." Our snickers earned us questioning looks from Elion and Laven as well as a knowing smirk from Aereon. Draveth just shot us a glare from inside the baggy white flannel. So attired, we all set out on the road again, hoping to make it out of the pass that day.

13
REACHING THE GOLDEN PLAINS

When Aereon brought us to a halt that evening, we were just past the end of the pass and the Golden Plains were in sight below us. I had never seen a more inviting sight. If I ignored the fact that we had kept moving forward this entire time, I could almost imagine that we had returned home somehow. The snow continued about halfway down the shoulder of the mountain we were on and then gradually gave way to fields that had already been harvested for the year and lay waiting for the next year's crop to be sown. Here and there were wooded areas and off to the left, almost to the horizon, a forest began that curved around the fields and the sporadic dots that were no doubt homes set on farmland with families inside preparing for winter. We made our camp that night in a small clearing just off the road and went to bed looking forward to the next day with a renewed hope that the worst was behind us.

Setting out the following morning, we all had a fresh spring in our step even though we were in an unfamiliar land. The farther from the mountains we journeyed, the more signs of life we saw all around us. Farmers went about mending their fences while their children cared for animals, some of which we had not seen the like of before. Back home, all of our milk came from goats since they were small enough that they could be kept almost anywhere and fed whatever scraps were left from the table. Here they apparently got their milk from great beasts that were two or three times the size of a man. Yet, for all of the size of these beasts and the horns that sometimes grew from their heads, they appeared to be docile enough that they wouldn't hurt a fly. They even came in different colors! Over here there were dark brown ones almost the color of bare dirt. Over yonder they were a light tan, like freshly scraped deer leather. The ones that looked to be the best cared for had splotches of black and white all over them. These black and white ones had the most people caring for them; maybe it was because they were two different colors? Extra people for extra colors? When I mentioned this to Aereon, he just threw his head back and roared with laughter. Aetheon overheard me and said that he wasn't sure but they sure did taste good.

We stopped at each of the small villages along the way and asked at the local market about the possibility of buying some seeds and were told that there were none available but we might try further down the road. The people we met were simple but likeable people who treated us well, if a bit warily at first. The first two nights we stopped, we were forced to camp outside of town because there simply was no inn to stay at. The third night, however, we hit it lucky in that there was an inn with beds for each of us and the price was decent enough. We all sank down gratefully on the beds and were asleep almost immediately when our heads touched the pillows. Just as I was drifting off, I thought I heard a horse neighing in the night but as it was from the wrong direction and much too far away to be one of ours, I did not dwell upon it. I was quickly off to sleep and dreaming about starry nights and laughing purple eyes again.

The next morning, we set out for our fourth day of riding through the fields along the road, certain in the knowledge that today was the day we would find a place that could sell us seeds. I knew that we must succeed soon as I could see the dark clouds gathering over and through the Forgotten Mountains, promising more snow than we could easily handle for the trip back. I shuddered at the thought of what a trip back over that same road with another foot or two of snow would be like. But our only other option was to stay where we were until the spring, but that would mean next year's crop would go into the ground late and be small when it was finally harvested. We could not afford to be caught here throughout the winter months. When I explained my thoughts to Aereon, he looked me in the eyes with a grim set to his mouth and said, "If it comes down to it, we'll take the shorter road and hope for the best. But I won't send us down that path unless I absolutely have to, you can be certain of that."

I took his words to heart. I just needed to know he had a plan in case things started to turn bad; now I wish I'd known how bad things would get. That morning was much the same as the previous three: we would ride into town, ask about seeds and be told there were none available. It was only after we stopped for lunch that things changed and not, apparently, for the better. We were riding along in our usual pattern when I saw Aereon perk up a bit in his saddle. I started looking around and then noticed that all the birds in the trees had gone quiet or flown away. A small hopping thing went racing from one side of the road to the other and from the corner of my eye I saw Aetheon's hand creeping toward his sword in its scabbard. I watched the trees as closely as I could without staring when suddenly I saw a face looking back at me over the top of an arrow. At a strange sort of whistle, two people stepped out onto the road in front of Aereon and Draveth's horses, holding up a hand for them to stop. Draveth looked startled and a bit indignant at being stopped so abruptly, but then he closed his mouth on whatever he was about to say as four more men and two women stepped out beside the first two, all six of them armed. Two of the men had drawn swords and the other two men along with the women had bows ready to fire and aimed at our group. I wondered how they planned to cover us all when I notice that at least ten more people had stepped out from the trees. Each was armed with their weapons pointed at one of our number. I risked a glance behind me and saw three others that I was not previously aware of back there. When Aereon noticed where Aetheon's hand was heading he got his attention and motioned for him to not do it. It is to the credit of their relationship that Aetheon did not question his brother but simply did as he asked. Looking around, I could see at least six people visibly relax when Aetheon moved his hand away from his sword.

Just as I was beginning to wonder how long we would be sitting there before we were killed or let go, two of the strangers, a man and a woman, looked at each other and when the woman jerked her head in the direction of the road, four of the strangers lowered their weapons and ducked into the woods. They emerged a short time later leading enough horses that everyone had their own mount. As each of the strangers mounted up, the woman who had gestured down the road turned to us and said, "Follow us and don't try to run. If you run, we will chase you down and kill you. Don't ask questions either. You will either figure things out on your own or be ignorant when we arrive. Come!" Then she turned and rode off in the same direction we had been going but faster and with more purpose than we had. We followed suit and took the same turns and twists in the road that she did. She steadily gained ground on us but never enough that we lost sight of her. Taking a chance that no one could hear quiet words over the sounds of the horses, I chanced to ask Aetheon if he knew where we were going. His louder voice replying, "I think so, but the people were a lot friendlier last time if I'm right," got several bows and swords pointed at us. I slowly held up my hands and gestured as if to say, "Okay, I'm done talking," which seemed to mollify them somewhat.

When sunset came, everyone dismounted, but instead of being allowed to set up a camp, the six of us were tied by our wrists to a long rope that was then looped around one of the stranger's feet. We were just close enough to the fire to stay warm but not close enough to be able to burn through the ropes holding us. When we awoke in the morning, it was immediately clear that several of the people who had captured us had been replaced by people who would accompany us to wherever we were being taken. The same woman from the day before used a knife to cut the long rope into sections that were tied to saddles and we were unceremoniously hoisted onto saddles. The ride was hard, but by midday we could see a large town or a small city off in the distance. It had a high wall so we could not see much of it, but it was clear that it was our destination.

By late afternoon, we had drawn close enough to the town to see the gate we would enter through and the throngs of people who had come out to meet the returning party. From what I had been able to overhear, the group escorting us had heard about a party coming through the mountains and asking about seeds so they were sent to investigate and return with us. It was a bit reassuring to know that they were supposed to return with us and not kill us on the spot, but I would still rather have my hands free.

Entering the city itself was a bit like what I thought Hodswell must have been like before everyone was gone. It was a riot of sights and sounds and smells the likes of which I had never before experienced. People were all over the place, packed in like sardines and fine with it, or so it seemed. I kept expecting to see someone with purple eyes for some reason and was almost disappointed when I didn't. After more than an hour of slow going as we moved through the streets, the woman in charge called a halt to the entire procession. All of the strangers then got down from their horses and drew their weapons again. I thought, here we go again, but wisely didn't say anything. Not even with the expression on my face.

14
BARGAINING

Looking around at the faces of the people who held bows and swords pointed at us, I felt that this was bound to be our end. I heard a sound start to emerge from Draveth and looked over to see him shifting in his saddle as if offended by the display of hostility we were being subjected to. I wasn't the only one to notice as at least half of the arrows pointed in our direction shifted to point straight at him. You could have heard a mouse fart in the silence that followed until I quietly whispered, "Draveth, don't move or open your mouth," with all of the authority I could muster at that moment. Either my words or my tone caused him to stop with his mouth hanging open and the words he was about to say died on his lips. I slowly raised my hands and waited until one of the town folk reached up and grabbed the reins of my horse to lead it further into the town square where everyone could get a look at me. Each of us was led in the same way and stopped in front of a severe looking group of men. When we stopped, two of the men with swords jabbed at us with the points to herd us down to the ground before the horses and wagons were led away to who knows where.

Each of our group was lined up in a row before the old men, who paced along the line looking us up and down, scrutinizing us as though we were some strange sort of creature that would either be kept or killed. When they were done looking us over, the men stepped away to talk among themselves. At times the discussion included gestures toward the Forgotten Mountains and at one point a man shouted, "Just take their stuff and be done with it, if that's the way you want to be." My pulse quickened a bit at that as I realized we had all just assumed that the people here would be glad to see us arrive. My palms started to get clammy as I thought how much easier it would be to just kill us and take our stuff than it would be to trade with us. The more I thought about it, the more nervous I got until I couldn't keep quiet any more.

In a voice that only squeaked a little bit I said, "We don't mean you any harm. We came to trade for seeds to get our crops going again. Our own crops were destroyed this year and without new seeds we won't have anything to plant next year." At this, some looked intrigued, so I continued gamely, "We can pay and now that we know you're here we can come back to trade on a regular basis." At this Draveth's eyes lit up while several of the men and women around us began to snicker or outright laugh.

Draveth was astounded at the villagers' apparent lack of interest in trade and virtually exploded, "How can you laugh at profit? You have things we don't and we have things I don't see around here! If we were to start trading, it would be more than worth the trip." By the time he wound down from his self-righteous tirade, most of the townsfolk were outright laughing and a few had lowered their weapons to hold their sides from laughing so hard. One of the women walked up to Draveth and poked him hard enough in the chest that he staggered, while saying, "You idiot, they're called the Forgotten Mountains for a reason. Nobody has had enough of a reason to cross the range in so long that everyone forgot there was anything on the other side. Those few that tried never returned and were forgotten in time as well." She poked him repeatedly as she continued harshly, "If you know what's good for you, you'll forget where you lot came from before you get killed trying to get back there." As she spoke her last words, she poked Draveth so hard that he fell over backwards with a stunned look on his face and sat there blinking up at her as if she'd grown a second head. I think it must have been the first time a woman had ever been so abrupt with him in his life.

To my own surprise I quickly intervened and said, "Be that as it may, we must go back, with or without seeds for a new crop. You can either trade with us and make some profit from it or we go back empty handed and nobody gains anything. Now, my name is Mykall, and I would like to show you what we brought with us." The woman looked flabbergasted and spluttered, "Didn't you hear me? You're probably going to die on your way back. Doesn't that bother you a little bit?" Thinking quickly, I replied, "Then trade with me and turn a profit before I die. Then, when I'm dead, you can have the satisfaction of knowing you were right and I was wrong. You can laugh about it while you use your new stuff." That brought smiles and chuckles to most of the crowd. One man in the back shouted, "Go on, might as well get 'is stuff while you can. He can't take it with him."

That seemed to defuse the tension a bit and most people lowered their weapons. The exceptions were the two men who had swords pointed at Draveth. They seemed intent on finding a reason to add a couple of holes to him. Much to my surprise, I found myself trying to help him. In a reasonable tone I said, "Most of what we have is gold coins to buy seeds but we do have some blankets and tools. You're also welcome to some of the equipment we brought to use on the trip if need be." At the mention of gold, the woman's eyes opened a bit wider and she asked, "Just how much gold did you say you had?"

Wary of a trick, Aereon laid his hand on my shoulder and countered by asking, "How much were you selling seeds for per bag? And how much is in each bag?" She looked startled and a little annoyed at this, which clued me in that she had been planning to demand everything we had while giving us little in return. By this point, the two men still holding their swords on Draveth lowered them and the woman explained, "My name is Ellerdril and I help run the farmer's market here. We sell grain seeds in hundred pound bags for three gold pieces a bag. Is this acceptable to you?"

I didn't like her tone so I told her, "At home, we only pay two gold pieces per bag. I don't think it would be worth more than two and a half per bag anywhere," then waited for her reply.

It wasn't long in coming when she snapped, "Then go home and buy it there! If you don't like our prices then don't buy from us." She started to turn and walk away along with the rest of the people around her so I reached out to grab her by the arm. When I grabbed her arm, she turned with a hand raised as if to hit me when I said hastily, "Fine, three gold pieces per hundred-pound bag. How much do you have that we can buy?" She quickly replied, "Deal!" with a gleam in her eyes that told me I'd gotten the worst of the deal. We walked from there to the farmer's market and there I saw at least forty bags of seeds stacked in the corner. A quick guess told me that this would be enough to start recovering from the loss of the crops back home but would not be enough to complete the recovery. I steeled myself and asked, "Is there any more than this?" One of the men escorting us was quick to reply, "We can spare no more. You can buy what we have or do without." I assumed they were lying but I was certain that they were going to refuse to sell us any more seed. Looking at Aereon and Draveth in turn, I turned back to our escorts and agreed to buy all that they had at the price they wanted. Once I counted out the money, they were all much more agreeable as the pouch with the gold coins in it was quickly made to disappear into a pocket for safekeeping. After the purchase was taken care of, the woman who was escorting us called for others to come and load the bags of seed in our wagons. Then Ellerdril turned to us with a smile and said, "Now that our business is done, we can celebrate all our good fortunes. You have to stay for the party tonight." Knowing we could not get far in what was left of the day, I spoke for us all when I agreed that we would stay for the night.

While we waited for the party to begin, Laven started wandering in and out of some of the stalls and shops at the market, curious about what was available. When Aetheon noticed that Draveth was sulking in a corner, he decided to join Laven. They disappeared into one of the shops for long enough I started to worry, so with Elion in tow I headed into the shop only to find it was the local armorer and the two were discussing the merits and value of different pieces. Elion laughed and said, "I think the trading bug may have bitten Laven a little." I joined in his laughter and we wandered off to find Aereon.

15
THE PARTY

The party that night was truly something to behold. Once the seeds had been paid for and loaded in our wagons, the townsfolk relaxed and started putting together a party that put our festival to shame. There was food being prepared everywhere including vegetable and fruit dishes. A wonderful smell began to fill the air that I had never smelled before. It smelled a little like the goats we used to cook up at home but much better. I followed the smell, and eventually the sound, of sizzling meat to a massive grill that was being run by four people and had a fifth person fetching more wood for the fire under the grill. People were coming up and getting small pieces of meat that were already done as a snack so I strolled up and did the same. The taste of the new type of meat was incredible. It seemed to explode on my tongue with flavor and melt in my mouth before I could even begin to chew. Where the goats back home were tough and somewhat gamey, this was tender and juicy. Being grilled right beside the meat were vegetables that I was mostly familiar with. There were peppers and onions and a few mushrooms sliced up thin.

The square was in the middle of being cleared out while tables were being carried in one by one before being set up in long lines with a large open square left in the middle. From the way one table had chairs set up only along one side, it was quickly clear that there were going to be guests of honor even though I was not sure who it would be. When I happened to catch Ellerdril off by herself, I made my way over and asked who the seats were for. She laughed at that and said that they were for us, of course; we had bought more seed from them than any had in a long time. She explained that while they often sold seeds, they rarely sold more than one or two bags at a time, so to sell forty at once was more than worth a party for the buyer. She explained this with a big smile on her face and a lilt in her voice that was hard for me to reconcile with the angry woman who had held us as prisoners for the last couple of days. When asked why they had treated us as prisoners when they found us, she explained, "There have been raiding parties made up of some kind of elves coming down from the mountains in the night. They come and go in the dark and leave almost no one alive. The fact is, the only reason we know they are some kind of elf is because one villager happened to be hiding from them in a haystack when he caught a glimpse of two of them. His gasp when he saw them was enough that they found him. They beat him so badly before leaving him that he died the next day from his wounds. When we found his body, he had managed to write the word 'elves' in his own blood on a board nearby. When we heard about a party of strangers riding in our lands, I feared you might be them. I'm glad I was wrong." This last was said with a smile and I could not help but agree.

As we stood there talking, the preparations for the party continued around us and soon musicians started to arrive and play whatever instruments they had. The resulting riot of noise quickly organized itself into lively dance tunes that sped up everyone's feet so that the party decorations were up much faster than anyone had dared to hope. As the last of the decorations went up, the decorators shifted over to partygoers and the party kicked into full swing. There was dancing that involved singles and couples swirling around the dance floor together all the way to complicated dances that called for the entire group to participate as one. I found myself dancing with many different girls, each more beautiful than the last. But one I barely met on the dance floor before she made her way off the floor and away from the party, seemed familiar to me. It wasn't until I really looked into her eyes as she glanced back while leaving that I realized they were the same purple eyes of the girl I had seen in Hodswell. Either she had followed us here or there were two girls with the same such eyes in this world. If that was the case, then I was in deep trouble. I watched closely as the girl with the purple eyes shyly pushed her hair up behind one slightly pointed ear before turning to go. As she turned, she moved into a deep shadow and I thought I saw her eyes flash to a glowing green for a moment. As soon as I saw Ellerdril again, I asked if she knew who the girl with the purple eyes was but she looked at me questioningly and said in a bewildered voice, "No one here has purple eyes; are you certain of what you saw?" I think that unnerved me more than anything. Everything else about the night was like something out of a dream and we went to bed stuffed with good food and good wine, having danced and laughed until we could stand no more.

Late the next morning, we got up and bade our hosts farewell as we needed to start back as soon as possible. They tried to convince us to stay another day or two but grudgingly accepted our reasoning that we needed to get back home with the seeds as soon as was possible. Our haste in leaving proved to be for naught, however, as while we were searching for a place to buy seeds the snow had continued to fall and the pass was buried in six feet of snow. We made our camp in the face of the snow and stayed there for a day while Aereon and Aetheon looked for a thinner spot that we could make it through and still take the longer road. They returned looking grim and told us that the only way we would make it would be to take the shorter road and hope for the best. So, the following day we rode to the mouth of that road and stayed the night there.

As we sat before the fire, Aereon got up and began to speak, "Where we are going is a place that can lead to some of the scariest things you will ever see. If luck favors us, then we will make it through with no harm to us. If luck is against us, then it is unlikely that all of us will get home. Along this road lies the turnoff to find the Grimm's enclave. We need to avoid taking that road at all costs. If they see us start down the path toward them, they'll kill us if at all possible. Just going past the turnoff may cause them to attack us anyway. Our best chance is to go as fast as we can and try to make it through to the other end in one day. The road is short enough that it can be done, but if there is too much snow we may get bogged down and have to stop for the night. If we do, we keep the fires high and sleep with our eyes open. Now, get some sleep; you're going to need it."

We all slept fitfully that night and rose early to get started as soon as possible. The first few miles were uneventful and I started to relax a bit thinking maybe whatever Aereon was so worried about was either not around anymore or leaving us alone. Things continued to be smooth as we went farther, even though the trees started to close in over the road until the sun was nearly blotted out. The snow kept getting deeper though, which made the going slower. Aereon and Aetheon got more and more on edge the slower we went until finally it started to sink in that they weren't worried we would get stuck. They were worried instead that we wouldn't make it out that day. When the sun finally started to set, we still had not even seen the turnoff that Aereon had told us about. Aereon, however, was nervous and jumpy as we set up the camp for the night. He insisted that we build the fire higher than usual and that we all sleep as close as possible to the fire. These alone would not have been worrying, but Aereon was the one who was most insistent that we take good care of the horses, yet tonight he insisted that we leave the horses saddled or hitched to the wagons. That concerned me until late in the night when there came a long, eerie howl that woke up the few of us who had managed to fall asleep. Laven asked if it might not be a wolf howling at the river when it went there to drink. I knew it couldn't be a wolf as we had crossed the bridge over the river miles before and this howl came from ahead of us and off to the side.

Aereon was remaining as calm as possible while he got us up and mounted before he started leading us away from the camp. When Elion asked if we should put out the fire to make it harder to find us, Aetheon insisted that they could see in the dark so finding us wouldn't be a problem. Aereon added that the fire might throw them off by leading them in the wrong direction for a time. Accepting that reasoning, we all rode quietly behind Aereon as he led us down the road with nothing more than what moonlight filtered through the trees to light the way. There was nothing more to do but wait and hope we could pass as unnoticed as possible. I feared that it would be a vain hope and waited for the worst.

16
FIRST CONTACT WITH THE GRIMM

We could see them lurking in the bushes, random movements of leaves with sickly green eyes glowing in the darkness. The pitch black shadows sliding through the woods gave the impression of things that were at least two feet taller than us as well as thin and wiry. As long as we kept riding, they seemed to be leaving us alone, but we all felt that things would change the moment they felt that they had the upper hand. As we came close to a fork in the road, the tension rose as the malice in the air pressed closer upon us all. I could see the tension in the furtive looks the horses kept sending in the direction of the trees. Aereon dropped back enough that he could reach out and check to see that the seeds in the back of the wagons were secure. When he was satisfied, he slowly rode back up to the front of the group. As he passed, I could barely hear him utter a quick, "Be ready to follow my lead."

When Aereon made it back to the front, I spread my legs for a sturdier balance and gripped the reins with white-knuckled fingers, waiting for some sign that things were changing. It seemed as if even the insects knew something was about to happen as they went eerily silent so that the clopping of hooves and the rustling of branches were the only sounds to be heard. As quickly as the silence descended it was broken as Aereon cried out, "Ride for your lives! Follow me and stay on the path!"

With that cry, the trees exploded into motion as I whipped the horses with the reins until they broke into a gallop. I quickly thought of swerving around Elion's wagon but just as rapidly saw that he had beaten me in getting his wagon to top speed. I was just getting the horses into a steady gallop with the wagon pulled along behind when I heard a cry from ahead. "Take the left fork! Keep to the left!" I could not tell who had shouted over the rumble of the wagons and the pounding of the hooves but I knew it had been one of our number so I turned when I saw the fork. As I turned, I must have gotten too close to the trees as I felt a heavy thump and the wagon shifted to the left a bit. Turning with my sword in hand, I held the reins steady with one hand and raised my sword unsteadily with the other to face a slender giant with glowing green eyes burning with a deep-seated hatred of all things human. As it lunged at me, I jerked the reins to the left a bit and as it was thrown off balance, I took the chance to swing my sword at the Grimm with all the strength I had to spare. Glowing purplish blood spurted as my sword bit deep into the thing's neck and it fell off the side of the wagon with a barely audible whimper. From my position standing in a crouch upon the wagon's seat, I saw Aereon kill two of the Grimm with a single arcing blow without slowing down one iota.

While I resettled myself in the seat, I took a quick glance behind me where I could see Aetheon holding Draveth's reins to lead his horse along while Draveth rode hunched in the saddle. A quickly growing stain on Draveth's tunic gave proof that he had been injured to some degree. Aetheon was fighting off attackers on both sides while he led Draveth's horse up near my wagon and practically shoved Draveth into the clear space directly behind me before throwing the reins of Draveth's horse around the post at the rear of the wagon to free up his hand. I felt that I was watching an entirely different man as Aetheon was guiding his horse with his legs and feet while wielding his sword to great effect in his right hand and a shorter sword that he had pulled from somewhere with his left hand. I sat in awe as he dispatched one foe with his right hand while fending off another with his left before reaching across his body and killing the second Grimm with his right. I was so enraptured by this incredible display that I almost missed seeing the Grimm hanging from the tree branch immediately ahead. It leaped as I approached but I got my sword up in time to catch it in the side. It dropped with a strangled squawk and bounced off of Draveth, who rolled it over the side while screaming from the surprise. I noticed Laven climbing onto Elion's wagon after tying his horse to the back and quickly understood that from there he could help defend Elion and the seed while Aereon led the way and Aetheon brought up the rear. Just as Laven made it into the wagon, two Grimm leaped from the trees and landed beside him. Catching one of his opponents off balance, Laven pushed it off the back of the wagon and to the ground where my horses and wagon promptly turned it into a pile of meat and splintered bone. Laven then turned to the other monster and swung his sword upward as he crouched and slid under the Grimm's razor sharp claws. The Grimm died in one slash and tumbled off the side.

As we raced headlong into the night, I could hear the excited cries of the Grimm turn to frustrated howls as we slowly pulled ahead and put some distance between us and them. By the time the sound of their cries died away to a distant howl the ragged breathing of the horses had begun to sound louder and louder, letting us know that they could not run for much longer without giving out. Draveth's pained groans had also increased in volume and I knew we had to stop to treat him before too much longer. It was therefore no surprise when Aereon called a halt a few minutes later and immediately started giving orders. He quickly got a camp organized by having those of us who could walk gather all the wood we could and pile it into six large piles for bonfires. When the first couple of piles were deemed high enough, he had Elion get started lighting one that we could then use to light the others. Aetheon climbed up in the back of my wagon to see to Draveth while the rest of us continued to gather wood. After getting the six bonfires built, we gathered extra wood to keep them burning bright. Only after that was done did we break out some food and sit to rest ourselves. When I asked Aereon if it was over he looked at me, smiled grimly and said, "Not by a long shot." Hearing that sent a shudder of fear through me. It was only when Aetheon said, "Even Draveth did well; he took down two before one got him. But he'll live to tell the story himself." I couldn't help but quip, "When he tells the story, it will probably be ten that he took down." which got a laugh out of everyone, even a chuckle from the back of my wagon before we heard a pained groan. With the tension broken a bit, we settled in to wait for whatever else the night held in store.

17
FINAL FIGHT

Sitting in the dark, trying to get rest, was like trying to ride a horse backwards. There was no way any of us could attempt to sleep listening to the howling and screaming from behind us in the woods. All we could do was sit near the fires and wonder when the end would come. Looking around at the others I decided that, more than anything, I wanted one more day with these men, even though it was not likely to happen. I looked to Aereon and with a heavy heart I asked the question we all dreaded knowing the answer to. "Are we going to make it through this?" Everyone but myself and Aereon winced at that point and then waited to hear his answer.

With a grim smile, he looked around and said, "I honestly don't know. The Grimm have only ever attacked in the dark but we have managed to rouse their fury. All we can do is our best and hope that it is enough. What I can tell you is that I would not want to be anywhere other than here with you lot. Over the past couple of months, we have come together as a group to save a great many livelihoods on the Plains. We have the way to do just that in those wagons right there. Now we must protect them until we can protect them no more! As long as one of us still stands at the end of this fight, then we all have won!" As Aereon spoke, we all felt hope rising within us until even Draveth was sitting up and gripping his sword as Aereon continued to speak. "If I fall tonight then I know each of you will stand in my place with all of your strength and fight! Those things out there are fighting for nothing more than hatred and anger. You are fighting for your friends and family. You have a home to go back to where you will find family and love. They are almost upon us, now is the time to stand and fight!" At this, we all let out a battle cry and stood to face the darkness.

As our cry reached its loudest, the Grimm set upon us. The fiends stopped or slowed at the sight of the fires and that gave me my first good look at what we were facing. What I saw was a creature that was much taller than any of us with a trim, well-muscled body. It was difficult to tell if the one I could see was male or female through the thick hides that it wore around the torso and down the legs to just above the knees. Each of its long-fingered hands sported claws that looked long and sharp, though not well cared for. Each hand held a long dagger that would be considered a sword were it in the hands of another. As I looked up into the face of this demon that seemed to have crawled out of my worst nightmares, I could not help but be struck by the high cheekbones and long, pointed nose surmounted by large, glowing green eyes that slanted upwards at a slight tilt. Around the shoulders fell long, unkempt black hair, swept back and tied with a strip of hide to keep it out of the way. I remember so much about that moment because in the next I locked eyes with it and all I could see was hate and rage at everything. That moment etched itself in my memory to the point that I would remember that look, along with the thing aiming it at me, until my dying day.

All too quickly the moment was broken as several of the Grimm gathered the courage to brave the light from the fires and charged at us with a wild cry of their own. The first few were met by Aereon and Aetheon, who held them at bay on the side of the camp where the road we had been traveling lay. The rest of us waited near the wagons for the ones we knew would hit us from the sides. The first of them came through on the side where Laven and I waited. As they rushed at us, I lunged forward to stab one through the lower abdomen. It dropped with a groan as I pulled my sword free so I could set myself for the other. From the corner of my eye I could see Laven wrestling with his own Grimm and with the noises I was hearing I knew that the others were busy as well. Looking around for my next opponent, I was just in time to see the Grimm that Laven was fighting raise one of its daggers high to drive it into his chest. I quickly lashed out and took off the fiend's head with a backhanded slash. After helping Laven shove the dead weight off of him, I grabbed his forearm to help him back to his feet. He accepted my help with a grateful nod of the head and a quick murmur of thanks upon which we both turned to help the others with their own fights. Aereon and Aetheon looked to be doing fine on their own so we turned our attention to Elion and Draveth instead. Elion had just finished off one opponent and was catching his breath when two tall, dark shapes dropped from the trees and moved to help the one that Draveth was struggling to fight off. Elion and Laven rushed to engage one of the newcomers while I moved to distract the other. While I circled my opponent, Elion feinted towards his while Laven rushed it from behind and ran it through. Circling my foe had brought me closer to Draveth's opponent without its being aware of me, so I stabbed it through the meat of the thigh, drawing a bloodcurdling scream and giving it a noticeable limp. Then I had no more time to devote to helping Draveth as I was busy with my own enemy, who had used my distraction to rush me.

I realized that I was focusing too much on the others when I didn't quite get out of the way in time and the first cut my opponent aimed my way sliced a gash in my forehead and left blood oozing down the side of my face. I could smell the coppery blood over the smell of sweat and the noxious breath of the Grimm before me. My sword was too far out of any position to be useful so I ducked my shoulder and rammed the tall elf in the gut. I put all of my strength into that one blow, which was barely enough to knock it backwards into the fire where it lay thrashing and screaming in its death throes. It was at that moment that I heard Aetheon let out a pained grunt following a meaty thud from his direction. I spun in time to see him stagger as the two Grimm he was fighting threw back their heads and howled with a mixture of fury and triumph. While Aetheon bent over trying to catch his breath, Elion, Laven and I fell upon the two howling monsters with a howl of our own. We beat those two until you could barely tell what they were to begin with and as we finally slowed to a stop, I noticed a dim glow above the trees. Looking around, I saw all but the most fearsome and determined of the Grimm back away from the light of a new day with a look of fear on their faces. As one, almost all turned and ran, leaving behind the few still fighting. What few were left went down quickly to our group so that by the time the first sliver of the sun was visible over the trees, we stood alone with our arms drooping and our swords barely held up by our hands. When it was all over, the ground was piled high with the corpses of our attackers and the dirt was a muddy mix of soil and blood, but the six of us still stood. While clearing the road, I took a quick tally of the dead and found that our little group of six had taken out twenty-seven of them before they fled from the sun. Aereon looked around grimly and said with finality, "We've made it through. You boys did well tonight. Now we just have to get far enough away today that they won't follow tonight. We move out in twenty minutes."

Wearily but relieved, we rode at a fast pace to cover as much ground as we could. All of us felt the bone weariness that came from being up all night fighting and still pushing on throughout the day. I felt bad when I almost nodded off for the second time but I felt a bit better about myself when Aetheon rode alongside my wagon all hunched over like he was about to fall asleep himself. While he was passing by, he started to cough and pressed his armored arm over his mouth to muffle the sound. When I asked if he was feeling okay, he waved his hand at me in a dismissive manner and kneed his horse to speed up a bit. Shortly after midday, we emerged from the trees into the wide valley that led to Hodswell in the far distance. We looked out over the valley, with its vast green grasses waving in the wind while the wide river flowed through it all the way to where it forked when it reached the far set of mountains. Once we had been in the valley for over an hour, Aereon called a halt so that we could rest the horses for a bit and eat something. As we rested he looked around and said, "We should be far enough from the woods that they will leave us alone now. We'll push on for a few more hours then make camp for the night. I, for one, am looking forward to a good night's rest, but for now, we push on."

After our collective groan, we got up and rode out. Even Draveth was on his own horse by this point. After a few hours that seemed like days, we stopped near the widest and slowest part of the river to rest for the night.

18
BROTHERS PARTING

The morning light brought a red glow to the horizon and a frown to Aereon's face. When I asked him what was wrong, he looked at me grimly and said, "A red sky is a bad omen for any traveler. Generally, it heralds the passing of someone close. The first time I saw one was the day my sister died. The second time was the day before my company found the temple where the Grimm kept their treasure. Both times it never occurred to me that I should have worried instead of ignoring it." With that he turned and began to walk towards the river. I heard the rest of the camp start to stir and glanced that way as Laven walked over to Aetheon, who was still asleep, and shook him by the shoulder. Aetheon partially rolled over and Laven jerked up with a frightened look on his face. He cried out, "Aereon! Get over here; Aetheon's hurt!" as loud as he possibly could. Aereon jerked his head around and started for the two at a flat out run.

When we got there, Aereon dropped to his knees beside Aetheon and finished rolling him on to his back so we could start getting his armor off. Once Aereon lifted up his breastplate it was obvious he had been hit harder than he let on. The entire side of his chest was covered in ugly shades of yellow, purple and blue. The bedroll Aetheon had been laying his head on had a large spot of blood on it and we could all see the trail of red through the gray of his beard. Hearing a strange sort of groan from

Aereon, I looked up to see his face fall as he stared at the wound on his brother's side. Catching his eye I asked, "What is it? What's wrong with him?" Aereon replied mournfully, "He's hurt inside as well as outside. I don't know if he'll make it or not," he said as he gently rolled Aetheon up on to his injured side. When Aetheon winced and started groaning in pain, I asked Aereon what he was doing other than hurting his brother. Aereon replied, "I'm rolling him on his side so that the blood coming from his lung doesn't fill up the other lung too. This way it drains out so he can breathe a little. Until we can get him to a doctor, that is about all we can do."

So, we quickly loaded up our gear and set out down the road with Aetheon resting in the wagon propped up on his side, which made him moan and groan almost all day long. Every hour or so Aereon called a halt so that he could check on Aetheon and when we did, we could here subdued voices coming from the back of the wagon. Occasionally, we heard muted laughter which was always followed by wet coughing on Aetheon's part. As the afternoon wore on, the look on Aereon's face became more drawn and haunted to the point that a couple of times I thought I saw tears drying on his face. With only a few hours left in the day, I felt a thump through the seat of the wagon and looked back to see Laven tying his horse's reins to the back. I locked eyes with him and nodded as he moved to Aetheon and began talking to him in a hushed voice. After about ten minutes, he moved to the place where he tied his horse and untied his reins. With only a slight lurch, Laven hopped off the back and remounted his horse. Soon he was back to riding behind Elion's wagon as if nothing had happened. I locked eyes with Elion and he mouthed the words, 'saying goodbye' to me, which explained everything. Looking closer at Laven I could see the glistening trails of tears on his cheeks. Shortly after that, Draveth rode up and, looking over the side of the wagon at Aetheon, said, "Thanks for saving me back there," before dropping back as well. I wanted nothing more at that moment than to knock him off his horse.

A while later, I began to hear more in the way of wet coughing from the back of the wagon and began to wonder how Elion and I would get a chance to say goodbye while driving the wagons. Elion clearly understood the situation too, as he called Laven to come up and drive his wagon for a bit. Laven climbed up without a word to take over and didn't make a sound when Elion rode his horse up to my wagon. Elion slowly climbed up into the back of my wagon and settled in beside Aetheon. When he stood up again more than fifteen minutes later to clamber up and sit beside me, I could see the tear tracks down his face. He said sadly, "It won't be long now. He's asking for you; go to him and then we'll get Aereon up here until he goes." With a heavy heart, I handed over the reins and started toward the back.

When I got to the back, I just stood there for a minute, rocking with the motion of the wagon as it rolled across bumps in the road, and looked down at Aetheon curled up in pain with the side of his face coated in blood from his mouth to his ear. When he noticed me standing there, he waved his arm a bit to beckon me to sit down beside him. I couldn't hide the sadness as I sat but said, "I'm here, Aetheon. Everything's going to be okay, you just hang in there."

He chuckled softly and in a quiet voice croaked, "Nice

try, but I know enough to know how this ends. I've got a little time left, but I'm bleeding inside and nothing can stop that. I'm glad to get the chance to say goodbye to everyone; dying in battle doesn't give you that chance. I've seen a lot of people go out in battle with a sword in their hand and I kind of thought that was how I wanted to go. But now, I think this might be a bit better." He stopped to cough for a minute. When he went on, his voice was a bit weaker. "Listen, I'm worried about Aereon. He's lost so many people in his life that I'm afraid he might decide it isn't worth going on any more. I need you to watch out for him. That old fool has a lot of living left to do, but he'll need a reason to keep on doing it. Besides, you were born for a life of adventure. I knew it from the first time I saw you in the pub. Aereon knows it too, he just didn't want to see you leave your regular life behind until you wanted to." I could see a bit of what he was saying and the thought of a life roaming around helping people definitely sounded better than farming.

As if he knew time was growing very short, he went on with a bit more haste even though it pained him. "When I'm gone I want you to have my stuff. The armor will need to be cleaned up but it is still solid and you can either use it yourself or sell it to buy new stuff. My horse is a good one and will last you a few more years. But the most important part waits back home. In a crate in the back storeroom of the pub is all the stuff I still have from the years Aereon and I were on the road together. None of it is his, so I can give it to whomever I want. That person is you, my boy. Use it as best you see fit. If my fool of a brother objects, tell him to shove it—he's got his own stash. Now get going and send Aereon up here." With that and a heavy heart, I pulled away and went back to take the reins from Elion. When I had regained my spot in the driver's seat, I told Elion, "I'll take the reins. You go get Aereon and send him up. His time is almost up." At that Elion scrambled back to Laven's horse and rode up to get Aereon from where he was at the head of the group. When Aereon dropped back to climb up on the wagon, Elion went back to trade off with Laven and sent Laven to ride up front.

Aereon moved faster and more nimbly than I'd ever seen him move outside of battle as he clambered up beside Aetheon and settled in beside him. He moved so quickly he forgot to tie up his reins so his horse just stopped without him even noticing in his haste to get to his brother. Laven grabbed his horse's reins as he rode by and tied them on the wagon without saying a word. I could hear the brothers' murmured voices from where I was and could not help but listen as Aereon said, "I'm here, little brother. Everything's okay now."

Aetheon whispered back, "No it isn't and you know it. You always were a terrible liar so don't bother trying now. Just tell it like it is. I'm dying. There's not much time left. And there's nothing anybody can do about it. If I can face that fact, so can you." He gave a quiet, rattling chuckle and said, "If our positions were reversed, I might be able to lie and convince you otherwise, but they're not and you can't, so there." He lapsed into a silence that was filled by a muffled sniffle or two from one of the brothers. Aereon muttered in a heart wrenching tone, "I don't know where to go from here. It's always been us together since we left home. What do I do without you to keep me out of trouble?"

Aetheon snorted at that and said, "You've always been the one keeping me out of trouble; I just keep life interesting for us both. Now you have to find someone else to do that for you. That Mykall kid is a likely enough sort for that. He needs you to teach him how to handle trouble and you need him to get you into trouble that needs handling. You're going to be fine, **B**rother. You just keep living and I'll handle the dying for now, okay?" I glanced back in time to see Aereon nod glumly before Aetheon continued, his voice growing weaker by the minute, "If you find yourself in the right part of the world at some point, do me a favor and stop by to see Mom and Dad if they're still around. I always wanted to get back to see them but the time was never right." He paused to cough more and when he resumed his voice had a sickly rattle to it. "I love you, brother," were the last words he managed to force out.

Aereon was openly sobbing as he held his brother's body close. As he sat there rocking them back and forth, he whispered, "I love you too, little brother."

I slowed my wagon to a halt while the others followed my lead. Climbing to the back of the wagon, I eased Aetheon's body away from Aereon's limp arms and gently closed his eyes. I found a spare blanket and covered Aetheon with it, wrapping it around him to cover him completely until we could deal with the body. I went back up and quickly moved the wagon out of the road before climbing down and instructing the others to set up camp while I dealt with Aereon. Draveth looked ready to object to me giving out orders but a single hard look from me was enough to silence his words before they even reached his lips. The others had already started to break out the bed rolls and Draveth was quick to join them. I turned back to the wagon and went to Aereon's side.

All I could do was hold him as he cradled Aetheon's head and wept for his brother. He glanced over at me and whispered, "He never wanted to be buried. To him, being buried meant you were tied to one spot forever and that was not a fate he wanted any part of. All he wanted done with his body was to go out like the Old Ones. We'll build a funeral pyre in the morning and light it up at dusk. That way we can celebrate his life by lighting the night and then move on in the morning." I looked around at the others who had all finished their work for the night and now sat quietly by the fire. We all locked eyes and agreed with no more than a slight nod that we would carry out Aereon's wishes without question. It would only cost us a day to honor one of our own.

So, when the sun rose, we had breakfast and got to work gathering the logs we would need for our task. By noon we had all of the big logs stacked and by mid-afternoon all of the smaller wood and kindling was in place. We left Aetheon wrapped in the blanket and placed him atop the pile at dusk. It didn't seem right to take the armor that helped to define him, so I left it on him to be burned along with the rest. Aereon insisted I have the sword though, as it had been in his family for generations and Aetheon had no son to pass it down to. As the last bit of the sun slipped below the mountains at the edge of the valley, Aereon lit the pyre and we stood to watch as the entire thing caught so well that the flames rose fifteen feet in the air. We stood there until the fire had burned down to a small flame and then to hot coals that softly glowed throughout the night. We slept around a smaller fire off to the side even though I was sure Aereon didn't sleep a wink all night. I asked the others and they confirmed that he had just sat there and watched the flames and then the coals all night. When morning came, I suggested that Aereon try to get some sleep in the wagon that day. Without a single bit of objection, he climbed up and slipped under a blanket. Disturbed by the hollow look in his eyes, I tied his horse's reins to the wagon and helped the others load up. I knew that, for one day, we could afford for Aereon to mourn, but after that we would have to move on. There were many days of travel between us and the empty town of Hodswell and then who knew what lay beyond that. I would have to talk to him that night. I only wished we could allow him more time to grieve. Setting out on the road was going to hurt badly as I knew that not only were we leaving what remained of Aetheon behind but that we were also leaving a piece of Aereon behind with him.

19
MOVING ON

The day after we consigned Aetheon to the fire, none of us had much to say beyond the basics needed to stay out of each other's way. Aereon stayed in the wagon until the middle of the afternoon before he emerged long enough to go into the bushes and relieve himself. Then he shuffled into the center of the camp like he was half asleep before sitting down by the fire and staring into it. Elion, Laven, Draveth and I stood there looking at each other as if trying to decide who would speak to Aereon first. I felt like strangling Draveth when he quickly spun and hurried off to busy himself with gathering wood for the night. I locked eyes with Elion first and saw confusion in them. I knew that while he had gotten to know Aetheon a bit, he was not close with Aereon, so I nodded to him and angled my head to the side to let him know that he didn't have to deal with this. With a look of relief on his face, Elion walked off quietly and busied himself with tending the horses. When I glanced over at Laven, I saw such a mask of loss and confusion on his face that I knew Laven was in no shape to help Aereon because he was still struggling with his own loss. Laven had been closer to Aetheon than any of us except for Aereon and he was not equipped to handle a loss like this. It would be some time before Laven was completely whole again. He had looked up to Aetheon like a second father and now he was lost without that father figure to guide him. He just stood there frozen as I made my way slowly over to the fire and sat down beside Aereon.

When I sat down on a smooth spot beside Aereon, he didn't even glance over at me; he just kept staring into the fire. We sat there like that for a while in silence. After a while, Aereon started to speak in a soft, broken voice that was almost too quiet to hear. The words he spoke broke my heart to hear. He said, "I don't know what to do anymore. I've watched out for Aetheon since we were little boys playing in the back of our dad's store. Without him, I don't know what to do. We've watched each other's backs for as long as I can remember. How do I keep going? More important, why do I keep going? It might as well have been me that died back there." He trailed off into sobs that left his broad shoulders heaving. All I could think of to do was lay my arm across his shoulders and hold him while he cried it out. It was nearly dark by the time he quieted down and slipped into sleep. I gently laid him down and covered him with one of the blankets. I walked over and joined the others so that we could talk about how to proceed from this point.

Draveth looked around at the rest of us and said, "We have to get moving tomorrow. If we wait any longer, we run the risk of more snow blocking our path. We'll just have to chuck him in a wagon and haul him along against his will if need be." I saw red at Draveth's callousness and since I was sitting beside him I stretched out and hit him in the back of his head as hard as I could. As he fell off the log he was sitting on, I hissed at him as loudly as I could, "He's just lost his brother; try to show some respect. How would you feel if the person you had lived and fought beside for decades died, huh?"

Elion looked up at the stars for a long while before opening his mouth and saying thoughtfully, "From the looks of things tonight and this afternoon, there probably won't be more snow for days yet. We can afford another day or two if Aereon needs the time. I remember when my grandad died, my dad needed a week just to get to the point of talking and working again." As he said that, Draveth stiffened and opened his mouth as if to speak but closed it again when I merely raised my hand. Elion snickered a bit at that and even Laven smiled a bit. I looked at them all and shook my head a little bit, saying, "We don't have a week, but I think we can spare a day or two for Aereon to get back on his feet. If that's not enough, then we will have to revisit the issue." This seemed to mollify Draveth a bit, and the others, while not exactly happy about it, were at least somewhat accepting of the time frame. With that being taken care of, we all shuffled off to bed to get some rest. While none of us slept well that night, we all got at least some sleep.

In the morning, we all got up around the same time to start our chores for the day. Much to our surprise, Aereon was up with us, but we knew he was not really there by the vacant look on his face and the aimless way he was walking around the camp. Not knowing what else to do, I invited him to help me with my work so that he would have something to do and maybe we could talk a bit. As we worked, I watched Aereon as he listlessly gathered wood until finally I gathered the nerve to talk to him. I started off by asking how he was feeling, to which he replied, "I'll be fine. I just have to get moving again and head back home. We were a couple of old fools to think we could do this. Neither of us was as young as we were the last time we came through here. I should have left him back home or taken the long way around."

I looked at him and with all the conviction I could muster said, "There was no way you could have left him behind. Watching him fight the wolves and the Grimm, he looked more alive and happier than I've ever seen him before. Leaving him behind would have meant leaving him to wither away to nothing in the pub back home." From the angry look on Aereon's face, I knew he wanted to argue with me so I continued before he could say a word. "Can you honestly tell me he would have wanted to go sitting in a pub somewhere with his face flat on a table? Or would he have wanted to go out in battle, defending his friends and fighting for a cause?" When I asked that, it took all of the fight out of Aereon. He hung his head and quietly admitted that Aetheon always wanted to die in battle. My next question rocked Aereon to the core. I asked Aereon, "What would Aetheon want you to do now?"

When Aereon said with a bit of conviction, "He would want me to go out and find a company to join up with. He knew my heart was never really into retiring, but I did it because he was dealing with old injuries." I asked him why he didn't just come out of retirement and find a new company to work with. He hung his head and told me sadly, "Because I'm too old now; nobody wants to take on an old man by himself. Without a good reason for them to hire me, I won't be able to find a company and will have to start out by myself. After a while someone might be willing to take me on, but it will be a long time before that happens." I felt sorry for him and a little spark that had been growing inside me burned a bit brighter. He was talking now and that was a good sign. I tossed an arm over his shoulder and pulled him a little closer, as though to keep what I had to say from being heard even though no one else was anywhere close to us. I said, "If you want to come out of retirement, you can start building your reputation again by helping us get this seed back home safely. Saving the livelihood of all the farmers will be talked about all over the Plains and word is bound to spread from there."

He looked sidelong at me and with a rueful grin said, "Nice line, but I get the point. We'd better get things ready so we can move out tomorrow morning. I know that no matter what happens, Aetheon wanted us to succeed and I aim to see that happen. After that, we'll see where things go." It wasn't quite what I was hoping for, but it was something and we could get back on the road. We finished gathering wood and headed back to camp. That night, Aereon wasn't his usual self but at least he didn't just ignore us and go to sleep. Several times he even joined the conversation, albeit with only a sentence or two. When we all lay down to sleep, I felt a bit more confident that when I woke up, we would get moving. The next morning, I woke up last and looked around, noticing that everyone else was already packing up to leave. Aereon was the last of us to mount up and when he did, I noticed he did it reluctantly. I understood why, but still I was grateful that he did it without complaint or hesitation. We set out for home and didn't look back. It hurt to think we were leaving Aetheon behind, but it had to be done.

20
UNEXPECTED ENDINGS

With Aereon beginning to ride a bit taller in the saddle and all of us in better spirits now that the end of our worst hardships seemed to be behind us, I felt a bit like whistling. A bit of cheerful banter had started to creep back into the conversations around the fire at night. The snow covering the valley itself seemed to be melting as there were patches of green showing through the white covering the ground. Riding through Hodswell itself, the emptiness of the city only matched the emptiness we felt in our hearts knowing that even if Aetheon's friend came back, the two could never meet up again. I don't know if it was the feeling of loss or just plain exhaustion that caused all of us to focus on the road and not on the buildings around us, but none of us noticed the time that passed. The ride back home passed slowly but uneventfully and soon we were crossing onto the rolling plains of home. Everyone perked up as we left the foothills and even the horses seemed to walk a little faster, as if they sensed that they were almost home. It was another couple of weeks before we made it back into town.

As we rode in, people who saw us coming spread the word so that by the time we stopped in the town square most of the population had turned out to meet us. When the first of the bags came out, a cheer went up as it was passed from hand to hand to a storage bin where it would be kept until it was time to sow. Once the fanfare had died down, things settled into a routine. Each day was much like the last as winter slowly rolled through the plains. Snowstorms came and left behind layers of white on the ground that all of the children had fun playing in. Occasionally, I would see Elion or Laven walking along beside a field. Sometimes when they did, I would see one of them stop and throw a snowball or two with a smile on their faces.

Draveth took to being back with ease. He went into his house mumbling something about sleeping in a real bed and no one saw or heard from him for three days except for the occasional loud snore. Once he finally came out, he strolled over to the pub in his finest suit and proceeded to start telling everything he could remember about the trip. Oddest thing was that in all of his stories, he never once mentioned being slapped in the back of the head multiple times by several different people. Whenever he got his wind up and started embellishing a tale, all it took was Aereon raising his hand combined with a hard glare to take the wind out of his sails in a minute. When Aereon wasn't in the pub or when Draveth was out and about, his part in the tales kept growing larger and more heroic until he was almost unrecognizable. His business grew accordingly as people would stop by to hear more stories and then stay to shop. He seemed at a bit of a loss though when he noticed that Laven was not hanging around him much anymore. Laven seemed to be coming into his own and looking out for himself first.

Elion was still pining over the fact that old man Ruthermon still wouldn't let him marry Erielle, even after we had gotten enough seed that the Farthing Plains would be saved. Elion would meet me in the pub on an almost nightly basis for a few pints of ale. During the day he would help me get my farm ready for planting in the spring and then we would head into town together on the nights when he wasn't sneaking off to see Erielle without her father knowing. The more time we spent working at my place, the more he came to love being there. It made me wonder if there was something wrong with me for what I was considering doing, but part of me felt better about the part of what I wanted that involved Elion.

Aereon was there, but he also wasn't there. Most nights he could be found in the pub drinking alone or with one of the farmers who happened to be there. One or two times when I walked in, he was drinking with someone in a hooded cloak. I thought it odd that anyone from town would sit in the pub with their hood up, but the few times I saw that person I was with Elion and occasionally Laven. Once I thought I saw the glitter of purple eyes under the hood, but I might have been mistaken. The nights when I sat with Aereon he usually bought all of our ale while he reminisced about Aetheon or sat in an uncomfortable silence. One night, Aereon looked up at me and said sadly, "Before Aetheon went, he told me that when I went back out, I should take you with me. He wasn't quite sure if you would go or not, but we both thought you might. He also said he wanted you to have his stuff. I'm fine with that; it was his to give and there's enough there that it should see you through no matter what you decide." I started to object but he stopped me, saying, "Don't worry about me. I've got more than enough to be just fine. Our last few escapades were very lucrative. You just have to decide if you're leaving with me or not. You have until the crops start to peek above the ground before I go."

I asked him the question, "Is it worth it? To leave everything and go fight for money in another land?" He looked me right in the eye and replied, "Worth it? I can't tell you if it would be worth it to you. All I can tell you is it has been well worth it to me. Each man who tries makes his own decision about the worth of this life. I do think you aren't happy being a farmer. You can either keep doing something you don't like for the rest of your life before dying in bed as an old man, or you can come with me and live a new type of life that may get you killed." Then he lapsed into a morose silence and wouldn't say any more that night.

I checked out Aetheon's stuff and was amazed at what I saw. The bottom half of the chest was filled with gold coins and the top half was littered with jewelry and random loose jewels. Laying on the very top was a broadsword and shield that were sturdy, with a few various pieces of armor under them. There was so much there that if I just stayed where I was, I would never have to work a farm again. I could buy or build a business larger than any other in the plains. I carefully removed the sword and reclosed the chest. That night, I got very little sleep as my dreams were haunted by purple eyes and swinging swords. Many nights after that were much the same.

Time passed and the weather slowly warmed, the seeds were sown and the farmers anxiously waited for the first shoots to appear. I waited for the same thing, but for a different reason.   When the time finally came, I had realized what I had to do. When the shoots appeared, Aereon announced that he would be leaving in the next few days. We arranged to meet for one last meal at midday out at my place since it was the furthest place down the road in the direction Aereon was going to be traveling. After lunch, everyone else followed Aereon outside without realizing I was not with them. They were finishing saying their goodbyes when I walked around the side of the house with my horse. Thinking I was intending to ride with Aereon for a bit before coming back, Elion looked at me and asked, "Why didn't you tell me you were going to see him off down the road? I would have liked to go along." Aereon looked away at his question while the others echoed Elion's sentiment.

I looked at Elion and said regretfully, "I didn't want you riding along because I won't be coming back. I'm going with Aereon."

Elion and Laven looked stunned while Draveth looked bored. Laven stammered, "But why?" at almost the same moment as Elion asked in a voice that was wavering, "But what about the place? Will you be coming back? Why would you leave like this?" Draveth just huffed, turned and walked away.

I went to Laven first, put my hand on the back of his head and said, "I'm going because I have to. I've seen too much to ever be happy with a life here on the farm. I need a life where I can do things that matter, have adventures and see new places." Then I hugged him and stepped back before turning to Draveth. His back was turned to me so I reached out and hit him in the back of the head one last time. He turned back around and started to snap at me until he saw my outstretched hand and grudgingly shook it. I told him, "Take care of yourself, and try not to be a butt about it." We dropped our hands and I turned to Elion, knowing this would be the hardest thing I had ever done to this point. I would have rather fought off a hundred of the Grimm than to have to say goodbye to Elion, but I knew it had to be done. I grabbed him tightly around the shoulders and held him while he cried. Then I held him at arm's length, looked him in the eye and said, "I have to go. This place isn't home for me anymore and it hasn't been for some time now. I would have you go with me, but you would be miserable. Your life and your future are here. I've left this place to you; the papers are on the desk in the study. With this place, old man Ruthermon will have to let you marry Erielle. You have a good life ahead of you here, Elion, and when I drop by to check on you, I expect to see lots of little ones running around." With that I turned and mounted my horse. Aereon looked over the group before looking at me and saying, "It's time to go." He then kicked his horse a bit to get it moving and started off down the road. With a final look around the farm and one last wave to my friends, I started off after Aereon, eager to see what awaited us down the road.

THE END

ABOUT ATMOSPHERE PRESS

Atmosphere Press is an independent, full-service publisher for excellent books in all genres and for all audiences. Learn more about what we do at atmospherepress.com.

We encourage you to check out some of Atmosphere's latest releases, which are available at Amazon.com and via order from your local bookstore:

Home is Not This Body, a novel by Karahn Washington
Whose Mary Kate, a novel by Jane Laclere Doyle
Stuck and Drunk in Shadyside, a novel by M. Byerly
These Things Happen, a novel by Chris Caldwell
Vanity: Murder in the Name of Sin, a novel by Rhiannon Garrard
Blood of the True Believer, a novel by Brandann R. Hill-Mann
The Dark Secrets of Barth and Williams College: A Comedy in Two Semesters, a novel by Glen Weissenberger
The Glorious Between, a novel by Doug Reid
An Expectation of Plenty, a novel by Thomas Bazar
Sink or Swim, Brooklyn, a novel by Ron Kemper
Lost and Found, a novel by Kevin Gardner
Eaten Alive, a novel by Tim Galati
The Sacrifice Zone, a novel by Roger S. Gottlieb
Olive, a novel by Barbara Braendlein

ABOUT THE AUTHOR

Casey Bruce is a science teacher of five years. He has a wife of sixteen years, two daughters and a white German Shepherd. His oldest daughter is twenty-five, they took her into their home ten years ago. His youngest daughter is biological and is fifteen years old. Casey enjoys spending time with his family, watching movies and playing video games as well as writing. Casey is a very loyal person with a strange sense of humor.